Dillon could honestly say there wasn't another woman of his acquaintance who collected bird's nests.

Diamonds, men and furs were generally accumulated by most of the females he knew. The things he was learning about Shay Oakland smashed every preconceived notion he'd ever had into smithereens.

Nothing had gone the way he'd expected since he took the tooth-rattling turnoff onto the rutted gravel road leading to her cabin, he reflected. He felt as bemused as Alice must have been when she slipped down the rabbit hole into Wonderland.

And intrigued, he added silently.

Dillon was definitely intrigued.

Dear Reader,

Welcome to Silhouette Special Edition...welcome to romance.

The hot month of July starts off with a sizzling event! Debbie Macomber's fiftieth book, *Baby Blessed,* is our THAT SPECIAL WOMAN! for July. This emotional, heartwarming book in which the promise of a new life reunites a husband and wife is not to be missed!

Christine Rimmer's series THE JONES GANG continues in *Sweetbriar Summit* with sexy Patrick Jones, the second of the rapscallion Jones brothers you'll meet. You'll want to be around when the Jones boys bring their own special brand of trouble to town!

Also this month, look for books by some of your favorite authors: Celeste Hamilton presents us with an emotional tale in *Which Way Is Home?* and Susan Mallery has a *Cowboy Daddy* waiting to find a family. July also offers *Unpredictable* by Patt Bucheister, and *Homeward Bound* by Sierra Rydell, her follow-up to *On Middle Ground.* A veritable light show of July fireworks!

I hope you enjoy this book, and all of the stories to come!

Sincerely,

Tara Gavin
Senior Editor

Please address questions and book requests to:
Silhouette Reader Service
U.S.: 3010 Walden Ave., P.O. Box 1325, Buffalo, NY 14269
Canadian: P.O. Box 609, Fort Erie, Ont. L2A 5X3

PATT BUCHEISTER

UNPREDICTABLE

SPECIAL EDITION®

Published by Silhouette Books
America's Publisher of Contemporary Romance

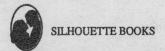

SILHOUETTE BOOKS

ISBN 0-373-09899-5

UNPREDICTABLE

Printed in U.S.A.

Books by Patt Bucheister

Silhouette Special Edition

Tilt at Windmills #773
Unpredictable #899

PATT BUCHEISTER

was born and raised in Iowa and has since lived in California, Hawaii and England. After moving nineteen times in the twenty-four years of her husband's career in the U.S. Navy, she has settled permanently with her husband in Virginia Beach—near the Atlantic Ocean and her two married sons. Due to extensive traveling over the years, she has a wide range of places and locations to use in her novels.

Along with her writing, she has a variety of interests, primarily painting in her studio and learning a form of martial arts called t'ai chi.

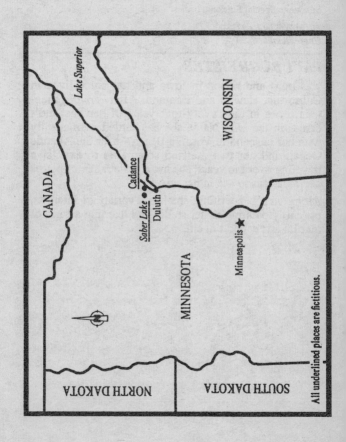

All underlined places are fictitious.

Chapter One

Dillon Street accidently bit his tongue when the right front tire of his rental car struck a deep rut in the road. The sharp pain did not improve his temper one bit. Or his language. The succinct, colorful curse word was for his own benefit since he was the only one in the car.

He was beginning to wonder if he was the only person within a radius of ten miles. The last vehicle he'd seen had been a tractor plugging along at five miles per hour until it finally pulled off into a field.

Dillon seriously doubted if anyone had traveled on this particular road since the Lewis and Clark expedition had passed through the Midwest. The trip must have been a real joy then, considering how much fun he was having now.

After turning off a smooth two-lane, blacktopped highway onto this graveled road from hell, Dillon knew after only a few yards that he should have paid more attention to Flynn. His friend had mentioned that according to the detective he'd sent to Minnesota, the lane to Shay Oakland's place was a little rough. Dillon made a disgusted sound deep in his throat. His friend had always been the master of understatement, but this time Flynn had outdone himself.

Calling this road a little rough was like saying a skunk had a slight odor.

Dillon wrenched the steering wheel to the right to avoid yet another yawning furrow and muttered another curse under his breath when the right rear tire sank into a narrow trench. And remained there. Rocking the car from first gear to reverse several times didn't accomplish a darn thing except to make Dillon's jaw clench even tighter. If that was possible.

He shut off the engine and sat for a few minutes as he weighed his options. All two of them. He could sit in the car and wait for someone to come along or walk the rest of the way. He had serious doubts about anyone using this road the rest of the decade. That left leaving the car for a little jaunt down the road on foot.

Dillon looked around. On either side of him, behind him, and in front of him were trees. Lots of trees. All kinds of trees. Tall trees and short trees with the first green leaves of spring filling out their branches. Bird-watchers and nature lovers would undoubtedly be ecstatic about such a display of the great outdoors.

As far as Dillon was concerned, they were welcome to it. Give him a noisy, crowded city any day of the week. Preferably San Francisco, where he lived. His sister damn well owed him a big one for this. Helping her with her little problem was a good excuse to get out of town, and he'd grabbed at it. It sounded better than running away from his own problem.

Dillon sighed heavily as he opened the car door. Hiding out instead of facing an enemy didn't sit well with him. He hated being forced to feel helpless and vulnerable and unable to fight back, even though he had to admit his friend, an experienced private investigator, had made sense.

"This guy is getting serious, Dillon," Flynn had told him. "And you'd be foolish not to take him seriously. I can't investigate the threats and the car bombing and protect you at the same time," Flynn had warned him. "I don't have enough qualified personnel to do the investigative legwork and be your bodyguard too. You could make my life easier and perhaps save your own if you'd disappear for a while."

With the concussion of the bomb still ringing in his ears hours after the explosion blew away his car, Dillon had decided to take Flynn's advice. So here he was about to mosey on down a washboard road to find a woman named Shay Oakland.

What he wouldn't give to hear the reassuring clang of cable cars as they ran up and down the hilly streets of San Francisco. Or horns honking, or street buskers playing their musical instruments, or some other normal sign of civilization. A bird sang from somewhere in the trees on his left, and he sent a dirty look in that general direction.

He took a pair of dark glasses out of his shirt pocket and shoved them on. After only a few steps, his brown leather loafers were coated in the chalky dust from the dry surface of the road. The moist fog he'd driven through earlier had burned off and the midmorning spring sun was warming the air around him.

After ten minutes of walking, he shrugged out of the black nylon taffeta jacket that bore his old football team's logo embroidered on the left front and his league patch on the right sleeve. He hooked the jacket over one finger and slung it over his right shoulder as he continued on his way. A few paces farther along, he rolled up the sleeves of his turquoise chambray shirt several turns.

Dust clung to the fabric, to his face, to his arms. He could even feel it clinging to his skin under his clothing. Feeling the grit when he ran his fingers through his hair, he could imagine how his trek along the country lane had changed the dark brown strands into something resembling dead moss. Fortunately vanity wasn't one of his faults. Even if he'd started out vain early in his career, having his face shoved into the turf on numerous football fields would have gotten rid of any preoccupation with his looks.

He looked down at his clothing. His British secretary had a perverse opinion about the proper attire worn by a successful businessman, even if the business was a chain of sporting goods stores. In a weak moment he'd given in to Beryl's nagging and had made a concession to leave his customary jeans in his suitcase for this trip to meet Shay Oakland. He should never have told her where he was going. Beryl Lovejoy was one of the designer's biggest fans and wanted Dillon to make a good impression. *His* idea of dressing up was to put on a clean pair of jeans and a pair of running shoes without any holes in them. Not this trip. The pressed crease in his pleated, light tan chino pants was the only thing that seemed to be standing up to the stroll through the rugged Minnesota backwoods.

Accidently stepping into a sharp depression in the road, Dillon flinched as pain shot through his bad knee.

"Gee, this is fun," he muttered under his breath.

His step faltered again when he heard the sound of several dogs barking. And they didn't sound all that far away. Or particularly friendly. A little late, Dillon remembered what else his friend had said. It was something about three huge dogs chasing Flynn's hired help to his truck, which was the reason the detective hadn't even gotten a glimpse of Shay Oakland, much less talked to her.

Let them come, Dillon thought grimly. He hadn't chalked up many points in his favor since he'd started this little trip. If he could face down three-hundred-pound linemen who had the disposition of ticked-off grizzly bears the minute they stepped onto a football field, he shouldn't have any problems with three little doggies.

He continued putting one Italian-loafered foot in front of the other and was rewarded by the sight of a two-story log cabin when he rounded a curve in the road. His first impressions were of gray weathered wood and teal blue trimmed windows. Behind the cabin was a horizontal streak of deep blue with glittering sunlight dancing over the rippling surface of water. Considering he was in the state of Minnesota, which claimed to have a thousand lakes, Dillon wondered why he was so surprised to see a body of water. All the fresh air he was being exposed to must be affecting his brain, he decided.

He brought his gaze back to the log cabin, which was in better shape than he'd anticipated. After the condition of the road leading to it, he'd expected something more rustic. Something along the primitive lines of Abe Lincoln's birthplace.

Pleasantly surprised, Dillon felt as though he'd just discovered the pot of gold at the end of a shabby rainbow now that he'd found Shay Oakland's hideaway. At least, he hoped this was her place.

His elation was brief.

He heard them first. Then he saw what was creating the rumble of growls and threatening barks. Between him and the cabin were three of the largest, scruffiest, meanest four-legged creatures he'd ever seen. Dillon stopped dead in his tracks, wondering if that was the condition Shay Oakland would eventually find him in when she ventured out for a stroll.

The movie *Cujo* sprang to mind as Dillon glanced at the thick heads, bristling fur and bared fangs of the three dogs lined up in a row facing him, an unfriendly barrier between him and the safety of the cabin. The intimidating sounds they made deep in their throats seemed as loud as the engines of three eighteen-wheelers.

Dillon didn't move a muscle as all three creatures advanced slowly, their steps in unison like a menacing chorus line. He didn't even blink as he considered his options again. Running was out of the question since the only place he could run to was the car, which was too far away. His days of shinnying up trees with any amount of expertise were over thanks to a knee injury inflicted by a crazed player on an opposing team. The possibility of Dillon's charming smile or polite conversation making any impression on the beasts was slim to none, he admitted, which left him with the only other thing he could think to do to attempt to defuse the situation.

Dillon began to whistle the first tune that came to mind, which was the theme song from one of his favorite Western movies, *The Magnificent Seven.*

All three dogs stopped growling as though someone had thrown a switch to turn off the sound effects. Two of them simply stared at Dillon with their ears twitching, their jaws snapped shut. The one in the middle tilted his head curiously to one side. Encouraged, Dillon took a step forward.

The dogs reacted as though he'd stepped on a land mine. The animals barked even louder, if that were possible, and with violent enthusiasm until a piercing whistle cut through their tirade.

Shay removed two fingers from between her lips when she saw the dogs had responded to her command. She didn't leave her position on the porch as she studied the man who was responsible for setting off the dogs.

She didn't need this, she thought wearily when she recognized him. A visit from any of her neighbors would be a nuisance this morning, but having Dillon Street pop up on her doorstep was worse. Until she could talk to him, she could only assume his sister, Amy Navarro, had asked him to make a personal appeal to Shay regarding her attending the grand opening of a Dream Street store. Perhaps if she'd had more than three hours' sleep, she would have been flattered Amy had sent Dillon to see her personally rather than send some anonymous member of her staff. But she wasn't thrilled, as half the population would be. She was irritated.

From the articles she'd read about him in newspapers and magazines, she had the impression that Dillon Street wasn't the kind of individual who took no for an answer. Personally or professionally. She would have to talk to him now that he was here.

She thought about what she knew about the man to prepare herself for meeting him. His escapades off the football field were as well-known as those between the goalposts. If her father hadn't been one of Dillon Street's biggest fans, Shay might never have known he'd once been a football player. He would simply be a man whose photos turned up in the newspaper and who was a commentator on the numerous televised football games her father watched religiously. She'd met his sister only once when Shay had signed a contract to design lingerie exclusively for Dream Street.

Her mother's agent had handled all the legal matters, forwarding contracts and payments for her creations, minus his fifteen percent, of course. There'd never been a reason for her to see either the owner of the company or her brother on a social basis. She couldn't think of any that would be bringing Dillon Street to her front door, other than the grand opening.

Although she'd never met him before, she had known other men like Dillon Street. She had had several of them as stepfathers, and it hadn't been an enjoyable experience. Shay didn't care much for the type. Arrogant, self-assured men appealed to many women, including her much-married mother. But Shay got along just fine without them. The way she'd been brought up had taught her to depend on herself and not other people, expecially not the God's-gift-to-women type.

She had to admit the photos she'd seen of Dillon Street hadn't done him justice. Even from a distance of twenty feet, Shay was aware of a powerful force drawing her toward him by an invisible thread. It wasn't just his rugged good looks, although his chiseled features and thick hair worn longer than current styles would draw the attention of any woman with an ounce of female hormones. According to the publicity she'd read about him, he'd taken full advantage of the fact for years. Now that she'd seen him in person, Shay could understand how some women would fall into his arms with very little persuasion. He had a way of carrying himself with an attitude of lazy insolence that certain types would find attractive.

Luckily, she was immune to men like Dillon Street.

Dillon looked in the direction of the cabin where the shrill sound had come from. He blinked, thinking his eyes were playing tricks on him. Then he simply stared.

A young woman was standing on the narrow porch. He removed his dark glasses slowly, wanting to see her more clearly, absently folding them and sticking them in his shirt pocket. Sunlight gleamed on the strands of her blond hair, which reminded Dillon of the angel his mother used to let him put on the top of their Christmas tree when he was young.

That odd thought out of the blue made him wonder if he was suffering from some type of sunstroke.

He rarely compared women with angels. He usually gravitated toward the other kind.

The woman stepped off the porch and walked toward him with a slow stride that made his mouth go dry. Beadwork decorated her black shirt in a network of multicolored designs sewn in geometric patterns and hung on fringe dangling from two front pockets. Stone-washed black jeans clung to slender hips and thighs, but what held Dillon's gaze the longest was the sight of the bluest eyes he'd ever seen. They were the exact color of a robin's egg and matched the sheets currently on his king-size bed in San Francisco.

About five feet away from Dillon, the woman stopped and suddenly slapped the side of a denim-covered thigh several times. In a soft, melodious voice, she ordered the dogs to come to her. Dillon wasn't at all surprised they obeyed instantly.

Lord knows, he would have done the same if she'd summoned him.

All three dogs crowded around her, each trying to get closer. Their tails were wagging furiously, their tongues hanging out the sides of their mouths as they panted with excitement and devotion.

Dillon knew how they felt. He was practically drooling, too. It was like finding an exotic butterfly when he'd expected to see a middle-aged toad. He no longer wondered where Shay Oakland found inspiration for her creations if this woman was the designer's daughter. He was feeling somewhat inspired himself.

A thick braid of blond hair fell forward when she bent her head to glance down at the animals vying for her attention. Dillon estimated the length would reach the middle of her back. The earlier childhood vision of an angel evaporated when he thought about running his fingers slowly through the long tresses once the silky strands were loosened from the confining braid.

His breath caught when she raised her gaze to meet his and her startling blue eyes looked directly at him. As Dillon noticed the humor in her gaze, he also detected exhaustion in their depths, a long-term weariness, not the temporary fatigue from a single late night on the town. He knew the difference. He'd seen both expressions in his bathroom mirror.

Stepping toward him, she instructed softly in an even tone, "If you'll hold out your hand, Mr. Street, and touch mine, the dogs will know you're welcome here. If they see I've accepted you, they will, too."

He shifted his jacket and extended his right hand. Then he realized she'd said his name. "You know who I am?"

"Of course." She took his hand, wrapping her fingers around his lightly. "I'll try to make this as painless as possible. The dogs are very protective, and this is the quickest way I've found to make them accept strangers."

He didn't mind taking her hand. In fact, he wouldn't care if he didn't have to let go for at least twenty-four hours. The back of her hand was as smooth and cool as satin, yet her palm and fingers indicated she didn't sit around manicuring her nails. His thumb stroked across the callused tips of her fingers, setting off a frisson of heat along his veins.

He was pleased to see the amusement in her expression fade, replaced by a look of puzzlement.

He wasn't the only one affected by the strange current arcing between them, he realized with satisfaction. Whatever it was, whether it was physical attraction, curiosity, or simply basic male-female chemistry, she was aware of it, too. He could see it in her eyes, feel it in her hesitation as she shook his hand. This type of complication was something he didn't need right now, he reminded himself. By the wary expression entering her eyes, she wasn't exactly thrilled with her own reaction, either.

He soon learned how she was going to handle her response to his touch when she pulled her hand free. She planned to pretend it didn't exist. He could see cool determination in her eyes. How could she do that? he marveled. He would find it easier to ignore an earthquake.

Pointing to the all-white dog closest to her, which seemed to be a combination of Siberian husky, horse and Saint Bernard, she said, "This is Chalk. The German shepherd is Otto, and last but by no means least is Lot, so named because a lot apparently went into his breeding. The saying about a dog's bark being worse than its bite applies to them. At least so far.

I'm not sure what they would do if someone attempted to physically hurt me."

Dillon gave the dogs a cursory glance, his interest more on their owner now that the animals no longer appeared to be a threat to any of his vital body parts. Her subtle warning was noted and forgotten since he didn't plan on harming her.

Beating around the bush had never been his style. Battering down whatever was in his way, maybe, but rarely ever tiptoeing around it.

"We've never met," he said curiously. "I would have remembered. How do you know me?"

"Doesn't everyone?" she said easily in a dry tone, which was no answer at all.

"Only football fans," he said in a tone that matched hers. "My days of being a celebrity player were over six years ago when I was forced to retire from the game. You would know about my exploits on the field only if you were a dedicated football fan with a long memory."

"Not all of your exploits have occurred on a football field, Mr. Street. You've appeared on television as a sports commentator for the last couple of years, and according to my father, who is an avid sports fan, you are a fairly good one."

He glanced around at the woods and solitary house. "You have television out here?"

"I don't, but a number of my neighbors have satellite dishes so you come in clearly. Occasionally, your picture also makes the newspapers, usually with some stunning woman draped over your arm.'' She grinned as she saw the surprised expression on his face. ''We do know how to read in Minnesota, you know. The last time you appeared in the newspaper around here was a couple of weeks ago when you were photographed with an English countess.'' She paused before she went on. ''Or maybe she was a duchess. The article hinted that she had made the trip to San Francisco just to see you. You were showing her some of the merchandise in a Dream Street store.'' She frowned briefly, then added, ''Or maybe it was in one of your sports equipment stores. I don't remember.''

''Lady Denham-Holmes dropped into the San Francisco Dream Street store on the recommendation of friends. My sister was busy, so I showed her around. She ended up buying a Lady Shay Victorian chemise.''

''A woman of taste, as well.''

Dillon heard the wry humor along with the sarcasm. He let both go by without comment. He'd seen the photo, too. Daphne Denham-Holmes had managed to give the impression she would like to try him on for size. He'd met a variety of aggressive women, but Daphne couldn't have been more obvious if she'd displayed a neon sign that read Take Me, I'm Yours.

She went on as though she hadn't expected an answer from him, anyway. ''I bet you've had many a mother hen clucking over her daughters and using you as an example of the type of men they should stay away from if at all possible.'' She suddenly frowned and paused again. "The reporter who wrote the article about you and the duchess mentioned a nickname."

"Lady."

"I'm sure you've been called a lot of things, Mr. Street," she said with a smile. "I doubt if 'lady' would be one of them."

"I was referring to the woman in the photo," he said patiently. "Lady is supposed to go in front of her name."

"Does it help?"

Floundering, he asked, "Does what help?"

"Calling her a lady. Does she act more like a lady than a woman who is a Miss or a Ms.?"

"There's no way I can answer that without damaging my reputation as a gentleman."

"Whatever," she murmured, then continued as though he hadn't interrupted. "The reporter used the name several times. Mustang? No, that's a wild horse. Maverick! That's it, isn't it? 'A maverick on the field and off' is how the article described you." She pursed her lips thoughtfully as she studied him. "A maverick is an unorthodox, undisciplined person. Are you?"

He was so mesmerized by her smiling lips and her line of chatter that darted all over the place like a Ping-Pong ball, one of her dogs could have nibbled on his ankle and he would never have noticed.

"Do you usually go off on conversational tangents like that?" he asked instead of answering her question, as if he could even remember what it was.

Her laughter sent tingles of awareness up his spine.

"I'm afraid so. A friend once told me I had a mind like a drunken jackrabbit, hopping from one subject to another without any idea where I was going."

Dillon couldn't take his eyes off her. The rush of attraction was as strong as the adrenaline high he'd experienced when he'd caught a long difficult pass and scored a touchdown.

Softly, more to himself than to her, he asked, "What in hell is someone like you doing living out here?"

Her expression was suddenly guarded. Taking a step back, she almost tripped over one of the dogs in her haste to put some distance between them. Dillon reached out for her, his intention only to help steady her. Pulling her against his long length hadn't really been necessary since she had caught her balance almost immediately, but he did it, anyway.

Lord, she felt good pressed against him.

For several heartbeats Dillon stared down into her fathomless blue eyes, momentarily stunned by the slash of need lacerating his self-control. Excitement and heat shimmered in the depths of her eyes, accelerating his own response when he realized he wasn't the only one affected.

He slowly released her when he saw wariness crowd out the awareness, even though letting her go was the last thing he wanted to do.

Sometimes lost yardage had to be sacrificed, he reminded himself, before eventually crossing the goal line and making a touchdown.

When he realized how strong his attraction had grown in such a short time, he wondered if all those collisions on the football field had rattled his brain. Getting involved with Shay Oakland's daughter would be utterly stupid. And brief. A long-distance affair might have a chance if he were an airline pilot, but would certainly be difficult under the circumstances. Hell, he thought as he watched her, it would be crazy.

As crazy as the way his body was reacting to a woman he barely knew.

Chapter Two

Shay took a step away, this time glancing back to make sure none of the dogs were in her way. Her pride refused to let her put more distance between them although her sense of survival would have liked at least ten feet. She didn't want Dillon Street to know she had been affected by his touch. *She* didn't want to know, either, but she would settle for keeping that knowledge from him.

She asked bluntly, "Why are you here, Mr. Street?"

It was a darn good question, he had to admit. "I've come to see your mother. There's something I want to talk to her about."

Her eyes widened in surprise. Then she looked down at the white dog who'd insinuated his thick head under her hand, silently offering his support or protection if she needed it. Absently scratching Chalk's ear, she asked, "What makes you think my mother would be here?"

"The mailbox on the side of the highway at the other end of the lane has her last name on it, and I followed the directions I was given to find her place," he answered, as puzzled by her question as she'd been by his. "She's two months' late with her current order, and she hasn't answered the last three letters of inquiry from my sister. She's an important designer for my sister's company, and Amy wanted to make sure she was all right. Amy was also hoping I could change Miss Oakland's mind about appearing at the opening of a Dream Street store in Minneapolis," he added. "The publicity would be beneficial to the store and to her. The Lady Shay line is one of the most popular in all the stores, which is why my sister especially wants her to attend the opening. All the other designers have agreed to make an appearance except for Miss Oakland."

The glimmer of amusement was back in her eyes when she looked up and met his gaze. With a soft chuckle, she said, "My mother has played a lot of roles in her career, but a lingerie designer hasn't been one of them as far as I know." She held out her right hand again. "This time I'll get it right. It's a pleasure to meet you, Mr. Street. I'm Shay Oakland."

"You're . . . ?"

"Shay Oakland," she supplied helpfully, filling in the gap he'd left when his voice trailed off into silence.

"You're kidding."

"I'd show you my birth certificate, but I don't have it with me." When he didn't take her hand, she raised it to shield her eyes from the sun. "I didn't realize you were so tall."

Staring down into her narrowed eyes, he murmured, "I didn't realize you were so young."

"In some cultures, twenty-nine is considered over-the-hill."

The dry tone of her voice made him grin. "For such an old lady, you've held up pretty well. I thought you were about nineteen. I could come up with about a dozen words to describe you, Shay Oakland," he murmured. "Over-the-hill isn't one of them." After a brief pause, he drawled, "You're late."

She blinked in surprise. "Excuse me?"

"Your contract stipulated you would supply Dream Street with five gowns by April first. Their records show they received only three."

"That's because I haven't sent the other two yet. Do you usually make personal visits to your sister's stores' designers?"

"I have to admit you're the exception, Shay. The other designers have telephones and actually answer them when Amy or her staff call. They even reply to letters sent to them."

"I answered the invitation to the grand opening," she said defensively.

"That's true. You sent polite regrets saying you had a prior commitment. Now what kind of activity could take place out here that is more important than your career? Couldn't a church social or wienie roast, though fun-filled and exciting, be missed just this once?"

"I was being tactful, a social behavior you might not be too familiar with, Mr. Street. I thought prior commitment sounded more polite than saying I'd rather walk barefoot over ground glass than attend a public spectacle."

"You aren't going to tell me you're shy, are you?"

"Not with a straight face, I couldn't. Would you accept private, instead? My designs are for public display, I am not."

Dillon studied her for a long moment. Then he asked, "What if I said we would have an opportunity to get to know each other better if you came to Minneapolis?"

Shay wished he wouldn't look at her quite so intently. She tilted her head fractionally to one side, her gaze direct. After a long pause she said frankly, "You're going to be a problem, aren't you?"

Smiling faintly, he said, "Probably."

"I'm not talking about business," she commented with a slight edge in her voice.

He held her gaze with his. "Neither am I."

With an exaggerated sigh, she said heavily, "And I was really looking forward to the first quiet day I've had in two weeks."

"Life can be like that," he said philosophically. "For instance, I thought I'd enjoy a peaceful little drive in the country from the airport. Instead I jarred a couple of teeth loose when I turned off the highway, and some of my vertebrae have probably compressed to make me two inches shorter than when I started that roller-coaster ride that passes as a road to your cabin. I don't even want to think about the damage to the rental car that is currently stuck up to its axle in your road from hell. Why don't you get your lane fixed?"

Instead of looking as though she felt badly that he'd been roughed up by her lane, Shay barely managed to contain a smile. "The rough road discourages visitors. Usually," she tacked on. "Not everyone is as persistent as you. Most people give up after the first couple of bumps."

"Why not simply put up a No Trespassing sign if you don't want company?"

She raised a single brow. "Would that have stopped you?"

"Probably not," he conceded.

"You just answered your own question."

"That road goes in two directions. Your lane has to be difficult for you unless you drive a World War II tank."

"I rarely use the lane."

He glanced at the large cabin, the trees almost engulfing it on three sides, then brought his gaze back to her. "Don't you ever leave this place?"

Smiling, she said, "You make it sound as though the thought of living this far from town is as alien as living on the moon. Until some enterprising entrepreneur starts a pizza business in Cadance that will deliver this far out, I have to buy groceries once in a while. I go into town when I need food."

"You could have solitude in a city by locking your door."

"And I could have noise, neighbors, and people."

"You don't like people?"

"Not in clumps with bony elbows poking me in the side when I'm simply trying to cross the street. I prefer peace and quiet and solitude." She chuckled lightly at his expression of horror. "Not everyone prefers city life, Mr. Street. I'm not forced at gunpoint to live this far from town. I'm here because I want to be."

Which raised a few questions in his mind. There had to be a reason why a vibrant, attractive young woman would voluntarily bury herself in the woods. Why that bothered him was another loaded question.

"When you go into town for food, how do you get there if you don't use your lane?"

"I use a boat."

"Doesn't the lake freeze over in the winter?"

"Very good, city boy. Yes, it does. Then I use the lane, but it isn't so rough once the ground freezes."

His gaze flicked to the lake behind her house. "And where does this boat take you in the summer?"

"To a dock belonging to the man who owns the lake. Quincy McCall lives only a couple of miles from Cadance. I leave my truck at his place and use it to go into town."

He brought his gaze back to her. "This guy owns a whole lake?"

"Quincy likes his privacy. Saber Lake is about three miles by seven, not very large as lakes go, especially in Minnesota, but he won't sell any of the land surrounding the lake even though he's had a number of offers. His cabin and mine are the only two residences with access to the lake. He wants to keep it that way." Her gaze ran over him as she changed the subject. "You seem to have a lot of my lane on your clothes, Mr. Street, and you must be thirsty after that long walk. If you'd like to come inside, I can give you something cool to drink before you leave."

"I can't leave. I told you. My car is stuck in your lane."

"Then we'll have to get it towed. Do you want something to drink first or not?"

"How can I refuse such a sweet invitation?"

"Very easily by saying no." Turning, she walked toward the house, the three dogs trailing closely behind her. She didn't look back to see if he was following her or not.

For a few seconds Dillon watched the way her slim hips moved subtly with each step she took. Shay Oakland had the most provocative walk Dillon had ever seen. He hesitated to follow her, feeling a strange premonition that his next step might very well be the most dangerous one of his life. Especially if he went toward Shay instead of away from her.

No one had called him a coward since Buster Miner in the third grade, and Dillon had given him a black eye. He wasn't about to call himself one, either.

But if she thought he was going to meekly leave after gulping down a cool drink, he thought as he followed her, she was going to get her first taste of his particular brand of stubbornness.

He realized she was wearing leather loafers when he heard the hard heels on the wooden steps leading up to the blue front door. Their scuffed appearance went with the territory, he decided as he glanced down at his own dust-covered shoes. The hefty lumberjack persona he'd originally pictured in his mind for Shay Oakland certainly didn't fit this woman. He'd be wise to stop making assumptions about her now that he'd met her.

Passing a blue painted Adirondack chair situated near the front door, he smiled faintly. So much for not making assumptions. He had automatically leapt at the idea that a single chair meant she lived alone. One chair and the lack of a gold band on her left hand didn't mean she didn't have a male roommate. Although she'd said only she and the owner of the lake lived in the area, he recalled. That didn't mean this Quincy guy and Shay were just neighbors. It was impossible for Dillon to imagine Shay not being involved with a man.

The spring hinge on the screen door squeaked in minor protest when Shay pulled it open. Dillon was only three steps behind her. The dogs, he was pleased to see, remained outside, lined up at the top of the steps with their gazes toward the lane.

Probably waiting for their next victim, he thought sourly.

Stopping just inside the doorway, Dillon looked around. His first impression was that he was still outside. Sunlight poured into the room through the wide, multiple windows, which were unencumbered by curtains. Long, slender, dry grapevines were stretched and intertwined to form a valance over each window and in no way interfered with the view of the lake or the sunlight pouring in.

With a sweeping glance of the large room, Dillon took in the heavy exposed beams crisscrossing overhead, natural wood walls, and blue wicker furniture, which consisted of a love seat and two chairs grouped loosely around a large, circular low table.

Shay motioned toward the grouping of furniture. "If you'd like to sit down, you don't need to be concerned about getting the furniture dusty. It'll brush off. If you would like to wash up, the bathroom is the first door on your right down the hall."

"Running water?" he commented with a single raised brow. "Like turning on a faucet and wet stuff comes out? I'm impressed. I thought I'd have to go down to the lake and fight off the fishies so I could wash my hands."

"All the comforts of home, city boy," she drawled. "You won't even have to pump a handle to bring the water up from a well or walk out back to an outhouse. The cabin has a septic tank and a generator for electricity. However, my selection of beverages is limited. Your choices are water, iced tea, lemonade or orange juice. I could make a pot of coffee if you prefer it. Take your pick."

"Water will be fine." His answer was automatic and distracted, his attention caught by the unusual contents of a large hutch against the far wall. "Are those bird nests?" He stepped closer, stopping in front of the open shelves above low cupboard doors. "These are bird nests," he confirmed in an accusing tone.

"Nothing gets past you, does it?" she said lightly as she walked out of the room.

Dillon turned his head around, unsatisfied with her answer, but she had left the room. She evaded questions with a skill he could only admire, he admitted. Bringing his attention back to the assortment of nests in front of him, he acknowledged that he'd asked a pretty stupid question. There wasn't anything else the circular clumps of interwoven dried grass and weeds could be but bird nests. He'd just been surprised to see them displayed on shelves. Especially so many. There must be more than twenty of them in various sizes and shapes.

He could honestly say there wasn't another woman of his acquaintance who collected bird nests. Diamonds, men and furs were generally accumulated by most of the women he knew. The things he was learning about Shay Oakland smashed every preconceived notion he'd ever had about her into smithereens.

Nothing had gone the way he'd expected since he'd taken the turnoff onto the road leading to her house, he reflected. He felt as bemused as Alice must have felt when she slipped through the keyhole into Wonderland.

And intrigued, he added silently. He was definitely intrigued.

Shay took her time placing ice cubes into two glasses and filling them with water. As she turned off the faucet, she heard the continuing rush of running water coming from the bathroom. Hearing the sounds of someone else moving around was so startling, it made her realize how accustomed she was to living alone.

There wasn't just someone else in her cabin, she clarified. Her temporary guest was Dillon Street. She'd been thrown off-balance from the moment she stepped out onto her porch and saw him facing the violent reception from her dogs. Dillon Street was the last person she had ever expected to come to her cabin.

And the first man to ever make her feel as though the air around her had suddenly become electrified when his fingers had closed around hers. She'd only just met the man, for crying out loud, she reminded herself. Her extreme reaction was just from lack of sleep, she rationalized. And shock at having the man appear unexpectedly.

Maybe if she hadn't been so preoccupied with Quincy's problems, she would have realized sooner that the owner of Dream Street wasn't the type to take no for an answer. With so many other things going on in Shay's life the last couple of months, the letters from Amy Navarro hadn't seemed all that important. They had been more like form letters than personal correspondence, but Shay had meant to answer them when she'd had the time. There hadn't been any to spare for two months.

She should be flattered the owner of Dream Street thought enough of her creations to take the trouble of sending Dillon Street all the way from San Francisco to see her personally. It was a little hard for her to believe Mrs. Navarro would go to the expense of sending someone to check on her. She had no false modesty about her work. Shay knew her designs were above average and sold well. But for Mrs. Navarro to send her brother to Minnesota seemed to Shay to be a bit like sending a lion to take care of a tiny mouse when a simple barn cat would do the job just as well.

It wasn't as though Dillon Street was sitting around with nothing to do. Even though it wasn't football season, he had a chain of sporting goods stores to oversee.

The grand opening of Dream Street wasn't going to be cancelled or ruined if she wasn't there. There had to be another reason why Dillon Street would leave the fast lane in San Francisco for a gravel road in Minnesota. He certainly wasn't there because he wanted to enjoy fresh air and sunshine. Shay had never seen anyone less enthusiastic about country life. He was like her mother in that he had seen and done almost everything. Coming to Cadance to talk to a designer who was behind in filling her orders didn't seem the type of chore the busy owner of a chain of stores would take on personally rather than delegate to a subordinate.

Since it was doubtful Dillon Street would confide in her about his reasons for being in Minnesota, all she could do was make it clear she wasn't going to change her mind about attending the opening. All she could do regarding her overdue designs was to promise to finish them as soon as possible. Then she would take him across the lake to Quincy's and call Travis's Garage to arrange for Dillon's rental car to be towed into Cadance and repaired if necessary.

She had another thought. If his car wasn't stuck too badly, maybe she could pull it out with her truck. It would mean driving the long way around the lake from Quincy's, which would take some time, but then her obligation would be over, and she could return home and catch up on her sleep.

She rolled her shoulders to ease the stiffness caused by sitting up most of the night. At least losing a night's sleep hadn't been for nothing. For the first time in what seemed like forever, she'd seen life glittering in

Quincy's eyes again. She smiled faintly. The medical specialists wouldn't have approved of her methods, but making Quincy lose his temper had accomplished what none of the doctors with their numerous medical degrees had been able to do with their pills, their instructions, and their advice. Quincy could make the devil himself hand over his pitchfork when he was on a roll. And last night he'd been in rare form.

Carrying the glasses of water into the living room, Shay nearly bumped into Dillon in the hall. Along with washing his face and his hands, he'd made an attempt to brush off some of the dust from his clothes.

"I bet you feel almost human again," she said lightly.

Dillon didn't know about human. He certainly felt very male standing close to her. Her scent was only one of the things he was having difficulty reconciling with this woman who lived in the back of beyond. He was as familiar with women's perfumes as many men were with vintage wines. Joy perfume was not sold in the local variety store, he knew from experience, having purchased a bottle or two of the expensive fragrance. A small town like the one he'd passed through doubtfully carried a perfume of that quality and cost. Which left the question of where the bottle of exclusive perfume came from.

During the short visit to the bathroom to wash his hands, he'd convinced himself he'd only been imagining his reaction to her. By the time he was wiping his hands dry with a purple towel, he'd successfully managed to convince himself his reaction to her was simply surprise mixed with a great deal of irritation caused by the torturous drive up her lane and the snarling welcome by her dogs. His conclusion might be simplistic but was better than admitting he was close to craving a woman. This particular woman.

Now if he could only make himself believe it, he'd be a happy man.

He tried to rationalize the tension in his body as from recently escaping death and being forced to leave San Francisco because of some nut.

He almost had himself convinced until he looked into Shay's stunning blue eyes and felt drawn into their depths.

She held his gaze for a few seconds, then handed him one of the glasses before stepping over to the sofa. She nearly groaned with pleasure as her tired body sank into the soft cushions. Since stretching out and closing her eyes was out of the question at the moment, she settled for resting her head on the back of the sofa.

Dillon chose the upholstered chair near her. Taking in the shadows under her eyes and the slack relaxation of her body, he asked, "Did we have a late night on the town?"

"We had a late night but not out on the town." She tilted her head slightly to one side and asked a question of her own. "Did your sister realize what a big favor you were doing for her when she asked you to come to Minnesota?"

Dillon shrugged. "Since I got her involved in the lingerie business in the first place, I couldn't refuse her when she was worried about losing your designs. Besides," he added vaguely, "I needed a change of scenery."

"You were responsible for her getting into the lingerie business? The line of sporting goods stores is a logical choice, but a macho athlete into frilly lingerie is quite a stretch." She chuckled, realizing what she'd said. "No pun intended."

He gave her a feeble smile in acknowledgment of her comment. "It started out as a joke after I was injured during a game. As it turned out, the game was my last as a player. When I got out of the hospital, some of my teammates gave me a retirement party. The knee injury that had put me in the hospital had finished my career. The guys were joking around about what I was going to do since I couldn't play football, asking questions like, Is there really life after football? The sort of profound question only people who have a higher alcohol reading than an IQ score would ask."

"How did a drunken party get you into women's lingerie?" she asked silkily.

"I was never *in* ladies' lingerie." He took a sip from the glass. "It was actually a crack made by the quarterback when a verbal list was being tossed around about the things I excelled in."

She raised a brow. "And you excelled in women's lingerie? I never would have guessed."

With a pained smile, he said, "I believe the comment had more to do with the fact I'd seen my share of women in a semistate of undress."

"It's an unusual job qualification but probably entertaining doing the research."

"Mac was joking, but it occurred to me that I did know what men liked to see and feel on women. The more I thought about it, the more the idea seemed like a good one. Selling lingerie sounded like fun compared to peddling life insurance or sitting in on some board of directors' meetings being strangled by a tie."

"Those are your job requirements, to have fun and not wear a tie?"

"Something like that," he murmured, wondering if her half-closed eyes were an indication of how tired she was or how bored. "My sister's husband has a winery in Marin County north of San Francisco and spends a lot of his time tending grapes. She was excited about the lingerie business idea, so I put up the capital and we became partners. Then I started the sporting equipment stores."

"So you're more or less a silent partner in Dream Street?"

"Sometimes I'm not all that silent. What about Shay Oakland, fashion designer? That's not exactly one of the top ten occupations for a young woman. How did you become interested in designing lingerie?"

Before she could answer, she heard a familiar static noise followed by the police dispatcher's voice. Shay grimaced, murmured, "Excuse me," and walked over to the wooden cabinet on the other side of the room.

Pulling open the lower left door, she unclipped a round microphone and held it in the palm of her hand near her mouth as she depressed a button on the side. "What is it, Jewel?"

"Quincy just called in and is fit to be tied that the end-of-the-month reports haven't been done yet. Says you should come in right away to do them."

"Couldn't Brad or Yale drop the reports off sometime today? I just got home after being up all night."

"Sorry. Quincy specifically asked for you to fill them out here at the office."

Gripping the microphone tightly, Shay stared at her collection of bird nests although she didn't actually see them. Her thoughts were on the argument she'd had with Quincy earlier. She was being reminded of the promise she had made shortly after his accident to help him in any way she could.

Sighing heavily, she said, "I guess I don't have a choice. I'll be right in, Jewel."

She was biting her bottom lip when she shut the cupboard door and stood. She made a startled sound when she turned away from the cupboard and nearly ran into Dillon.

"Sorry," she murmured, "I forgot you were here."

"You certainly know how to make a man feel good, Miss Oakland."

"Don't take it personally, Mr. Street. I'm operating on only a couple of brain cells this morning. The rest of them are fast asleep, which is what I would like to be.'' She glanced at the slim watch on her wrist. ''I need to go into town for a couple of hours. Would you mind waiting here until I get back or until the tow truck can come out? I'll give the local mechanic a call while I'm in town to tell him about your situation, but I can't promise he'll be right out.''

''Why don't I simply come with you now? I can make the arrangements myself or we can use your car to pull mine out of the hole once you finish with whatever it is you have to do.''

''I don't know how long I'll be.'' She certainly didn't feel like explaining what she had to do and why she was the one doing it. That would also bring Quincy into the conversation. After their heated disagreement last night, Shay wasn't ready to discuss him and explain his situation. Nor was she ready to face Quincy yet.

''Make yourself comfortable, Mr. Street. With any luck, the towing service can come out right away. Then you'll be able to return to civilization.''

He didn't have the heart to burst her bubble when she looked so worn down by informing her he wasn't going anywhere. Not yet, anyway. Glancing at the cupboard that held the radio transmitter, he asked, ''Why don't you have a phone?''

She shook her head. ''I don't have much use for one. There was one here when I first moved in. After a storm knocked down the lines, I found I liked the isolation.'' She had to smile as he looked at her as though she was speaking a foreign language. "You obviously don't agree. I bet you even have a phone in your car."

"Of course." At least he'd had a phone until his car had been blown up. But he didn't add that bit of information.

"I thought so. Well, I'll try to get you back to the big city as soon as I can. In the meantime, you'll have to rough it here until I can arrange for your car to be towed."

Dillon watched her walk away. Nothing about this trip was going the way he'd expected, least of all dealing with Shay Oakland. He'd never met anyone quite like her before. Which perhaps was part of the attraction. Some of the other designers under contract with Dream Street could generously be called eccentric. Zina Inez, a former Las Vegas showgirl, designed stunning classical creations for Dream Street, incorporating boa feathers on each piece. Zena herself was a walking advertisement for her designs, leaving a trail of imitation ostrich feathers in her wake whenever she walked out of a room. Zena, like the other designers, thrived on attention and adulation, always agreeing to appear whenever and wherever she was asked to be.

Shay Oakland couldn't care less about publicity. His curiosity was beginning to stir up a series of questions. One that he'd already asked her but she had skirted around and hadn't answered. Why was someone like her living out in the boonies? Without even a phone, for God's sake.

The throaty sound of an engine turning over cut into his thoughts. Stepping over to a window facing the lake, Dillon looked out and saw a small speedboat cut through the smooth surface of the lake. Shay's golden hair seemed almost white in the bright sunlight. He continued to watch her until he could no longer see her. He had been attracted to all different types of women in the past, even besotted a time or two when he was young, gullible, and interested more in quantity than in quality.

But he'd never been fascinated by a woman before.

Turning away from the window, Dillon decided to put to use some of the tricks of the private investigator trade he'd picked up from his pal Flynn. It looked as if he was going to have plenty of time. He glanced around the room. This was as good a place as any to start.

Chapter Three

Hours later, the side of the boat scrunched against an old car tire that was looped over one of the dock posts to protect boats. If Shay needed any proof of her exhausted condition, she had it when the boat bumped heavily into the dock. She'd brought the boat in too fast. Her only excuse was she was tired after spending hours at the police station doing Quincy's paperwork.

After tying the lines securely, she left the dock, easily finding her way to the cottage with a little help from a full moon. She caught her toe on a tuft of coarse grass but caught her balance in time. If she'd fallen, she wasn't sure she would have had the energy to get up again. Sleeping on the grass didn't sound like such a bad idea.

Shay frowned. It had to be more comfortable than falling asleep at Quincy's desk. For someone who thought she was in relatively good physical shape, she had taken an embarrassingly long time to unkink her muscles after Yale shook her awake. The deputy had been amused to find her asleep, her head resting on a forearm spread across the papers she'd been working on in Quincy's office. Fortunately she'd finished the last report before falling asleep. Quincy would have to come up with something else to complain about.

All three dogs came galloping around the corner of the cabin, nearly knocking her over with their enthusiastic greeting. She half leaned on Chalk as she made her way to the back door, her fingers burrowing into his soft fur. She was glad she had fed the dogs in the morning. Opening up cans of dog food would require more energy than she could muster right now.

When she reached the back porch, she stroked each dog. "Good night, guys. See you in the morning."

The hinges of the screen door squeaked as she pulled it open, then protested again when she let it close behind her. In the back of her mind lingered a vague notion that she was forgetting to do something. Her tired brain wasn't cooperating though, and she couldn't think what it might be.

The beadwork on her shirt clattered softly in the quiet kitchen as she walked through to the living room. Several feet away from the bottom of the stairs, she began unbuttoning her blouse, stopping when her fingers met the resistance of her belt. She tugged the shirt out of her waistband and let the tails hang down over the outside of her jeans. With the front of her shirt open, she dragged first one foot, then the other up the stairwell.

She was completely oblivious of the man standing near the window facing the lake. Dillon had heard the boat's motor and the dogs barking when Shay returned, and had watched her shadowy figure walk toward the cabin. It was as though she was an apparition rising up from the misty fog shrouding the lake.

Her exhaustion was apparent in the way she walked, as if each shoe weighed twenty pounds. Another indication of her weary state was that she had apparently forgotten he was there, he realized ruefully. He might have only met her for a brief time that morning, but Dillon knew Shay wasn't the type of woman to start undressing in front of a stranger unless she had a damn good reason. Being half conscious would qualify.

This habit of hers of forgetting about him could become irritating if it continued.

Dillon didn't move until he heard a door close upstairs. Only then did he walk over to the couch. He wasn't looking forward to sleeping in his clothes on a too-short sofa, but he removed his shoes and nothing else, since a half-naked man might not be something she wanted to wake up to. Shay was going to have a big enough shock finding him still there in the morning.

He stretched his long legs out on the cushions and arranged a square decorative pillow under his head. It was only a few minutes past nine o'clock, and he was settling down for the night. He hadn't been to bed that early since he was in junior high school. Anyone who knew him would have difficulty believing it. Hell, he had trouble believing it.

The unaccustomed sounds of the night were different than he was used to and louder. He realized there wasn't any noise at night in his high-rise apartment except the ones he created by turning on the stereo and the television. His apartment was too far from the street for him to hear traffic below and soundproofed so well that he couldn't hear any of his neighbors.

Now he was hearing an odd assortment of noises, some recognizable, like the branches of fir trees brushing against the cabin, and others as foreign to his ears as hearing a bagpipe being played in his brother-in-law's grape fields. Dillon had no idea if the rustling sounds outside the windows were made by anything other than the trees. Like something with four legs and lots of big teeth. He didn't really want to know.

To take his mind off the thought of lions and tigers and bears roaming the woods outside, he let his mind wander back to the woman upstairs. He'd already figured out that she hadn't been able to get the towing service to come out since no one had shown up while she'd been gone. Or else she'd forgotten about his little problem. Just as it had obviously slipped her mind that she'd left him at her place.

Folding his arms over his chest, Dillon stared at the ceiling. The floorboards overhead creaked occasionally. Even though she was exhausted, Shay was apparently having difficulty getting to sleep. After listening for a few minutes, Dillon suspected Shay was pacing the floor when the creaking continued. Evidently something was bothering her, and he was more than a little tempted to go upstairs to offer his help with whatever was preventing her from getting the sleep she badly needed.

He'd probably scare the hell out of her since she had forgotten about him. His ego could take a few lumps as much as his body had during his football career. Having a woman forget his existence wasn't going to ruin his life. In this instance, however, it wasn't going to happen again.

Before they were through, Shay was going to have a reason or two to remember Dillon Street.

The tantalizing aroma of strong coffee was a subtle nudge to her senses, awakening Shay from a fitful sleep. Dragging open her heavy lids, she frowned when she realized she was wearing the clothes she'd put on yesterday morning. She'd managed to kick off her shoes before sprawling across her blue bedspread but that was all the preparation she'd made prior to lying down.

She felt as fresh as a week-old bagel and set out to do something to change that. The shower helped encourage a few brain cells into action, which is why it finally occurred to her that the scent of freshly brewed coffee hadn't been wishful thinking but the real thing.

She stared at her reflection in the mirror as she hooked her hair back with a faux ivory clasp behind her head. She stared at her reflection in the mirror over the sink. Closing her eyes briefly, she opened them again. Now she remembered what had been niggling at the back of her mind when she'd walked into the cabin last night. She had a visitor.

"Oh, Lord," she said under her breath, hoping against every logical thought that she was wrong. Maybe Dillon Street had been a dream and hadn't been there at all.

The faint sound of a door closing downstairs and the dogs barking contradicted her refusal to accept what her mind was trying to tell her.

Dillon Street was wandering around downstairs.

She put her hand to her forehead. How could she have forgotten him? she asked herself without any hope of coming up with the answer. She'd been tired, almost sick with exhaustion and worry last night, but forgetting she'd left Dillon Street in her cabin was pretty bad.

When Travis from the garage had informed her yesterday that he'd try to get out to her place that evening, she'd dismissed the subject of Dillon Street and gotten on with the work she needed to do in Quincy's

office. Several people had popped in to inquire about
Quincy's health when they saw her truck parked out
front. The mayor dropped by on his way home from
the Moose Lodge meeting and informed her that
Quincy's replacement would be able to take over as
chief of police on June first. She should have checked
back with Travis, but after the initial phone call, she'd
put Dillon Street out of her mind.

Evidently Travis never made it. Or Dillon Street was
sticking around to continue his campaign to get her to
appear at the grand opening.

Whatever the reason, he was still there, and she was
going to have to deal with him. It was too much to
hope that a raccoon had found a way inside and had
fixed himself a cup of coffee.

She tucked her white shirt into the waistband of her
jeans, fastened the silver clasp of a thin leather belt
around her waist, and pulled a coral pink, loosely knit
sweater on over her head and let it fall over her hips.

She dredged up a smile at the thought of her mother's reaction to her choice of apparel when there was
a man between the ages of twenty and a hundred in the
vicinity. Monica's idea of casual dress was to leave one
button of her suit jacket undone.

Once downstairs, Shay looked for Dillon in the living room and kitchen. Remembering the sound of a
closing door, she went to the front of the cabin and
looked out. Dillon was sitting on the top porch step
with his back against one of the posts. He was wearing his black jacket, although he hadn't bothered to

fasten the front. He was resting a cup of steaming coffee on his thigh as he stared toward the woods. Since he didn't look as if he was going anywhere soon, Shay returned to the kitchen to pour a cup for herself. Before joining him outside, she put on a jacket to ward off the chilly morning air.

Dillon turned his head in her direction when the spring squeaked as she pushed the door open, the expression on his face blank. Except for his eyes, she noted. His sable brown eyes were searching and curious as his gaze went directly to her face.

"Good morning," he murmured in a drowsy voice.

"Good morning." Shay sat down in the Adirondack chair several feet away, grimacing at the feel of the damp cushion on the seat of her jeans.

"I owe you an apology," she began.

"For what?"

"For leaving you here on your own for so long. I thought Travis would send someone out to tow your car. He said he'd try when I asked him yesterday."

"Don't worry about it." A corner of his mouth lifted. "I amused myself."

"You haven't been up all night, have you?"

He shook his head. "I stretched out on your couch."

"I'm afraid I was out of it when I got home last night. I didn't even think about you or your car."

Dillon watched the remaining coffee swirl around in his cup as he moved it in a circular motion. Then he looked up. "That will be the last time."

"Last time?" She blinked, surprised at the bite in his voice. "For what?"

"The last time you forget I'm around."

"This early morning country air must be getting to your polluted brain. You aren't making any sense."

"That depends on your viewpoint. If you need it made clearer, how about if I tell you I'm sticking around?"

Wrapping both hands around the cup, she said frankly, "Why?"

Her caution made him smile. "I think it's one of those boy and girl things. You know, kissing, hugging, stuff like that."

She didn't take him seriously. "Going through withdrawal after only one night alone?"

"Hell, no," he replied easily. "I've been known to go several days without a woman. Hard to believe maybe, but true." His eyes narrowed. "Does my reputation with women bother you?"

"Why would it?" she responded. "Your personal life has nothing to do with me."

"Maybe I haven't made myself as clear as I thought. I was warning you that we're going to be getting deeply personal while I'm here."

She debated laughing at his bizarre statement. She might have if she'd seen even a hint of humor in his eyes. He was looking at her with a simmering heat in the depths of his dark, brooding eyes that created a sizzling current of response along her nerve endings.

"No," she stated flatly. "We're not."

"Yes," he answered firmly. "We are."

Suddenly Shay stiffened, listened for a few seconds, then muttered "Damn" under her breath.

She'd taken two steps toward the door when Dillon asked, "Where are you going?"

"It's the two-way radio."

She was inside opening the cupboard door when she became aware that Dillon had followed her. Picking up the receiver, she said, "I'm here, Jewel. What's the problem?"

"Mr. Varanger is lost again. Brad responded to Mrs. Varanger's phone call, but she insists you come out personally since Quincy can't." After a short pause, the dispatcher added, "Shay, Mrs. Varanger mentioned that the shotgun is missing, too."

Just barely, Shay managed to restrain her impatience. Quincy had warned Mrs. Varanger enough times about the dangers of leaving the shotgun where her husband could reach it, but the elderly woman refused to believe Arnold would hurt anyone. At one time he wouldn't have, but now his illness made him unpredictable.

"Is Brad contacting the neighbors to see if they've seen Mr. Varanger?"

"He's doing that now."

"Have you notified Quincy?"

"I did that right away. He told me to call you."

She sighed. "I'll be there as soon as I can."

She replaced the microphone and opened the other cupboard door. "You can ride with me to Quincy's," she told Dillon as she reached inside. "He has a phone. You can call for a tow from his place."

He'd be damned if he'd be dismissed so easily. "Thanks anyway, but I'll wait here. I can call the garage myself. When you get back, we can continue the interesting discussion we were having on the porch."

She stared at him, then shook her head several times, a bemused smile curving her mouth. "You don't give up, do you?"

"Not when there's something I want."

"There are a couple of flaws in your plan."

"Like what?"

"Well. For one thing, you're never going to get your car out of the lane this way. I have no idea how long I'll be, so you had better come with me to Quincy's and use his phone if you want to badger the towing company."

"I'm not leaving until we get a few things clear between us."

She didn't argue with him. "Suit yourself. I don't have time to argue with you right now." She kept her gaze on his face as she hooked an object on her belt on the right side of her waist.

It was a small holster with a gun tucked inside.

Chapter Four

Dillon liked to think he could take a joke as well as the next guy, but he didn't find this one remotely funny. He sincerely hoped the gun was made out of rubber. It looked very real, however, and he was highly nervous about such deadly items since his car had been blown up.

"What the hell is going on?" he snapped, his body tense, his eyes narrowed as he stared at the lethal weapon.

Shay had clipped Quincy's gun on because it was easier to wear than to carry while she operated the boat. The fact that the sight of the gun had caused an unusual response from Dillon was interesting. It hadn't been intentional, but she felt a small satisfaction in rattling his calm exterior. Instead of being intimidated, however, he was angry, not frightened, or even surprised, but furious for some reason. Shay also got the impression every muscle in his body was tense like a soldier preparing for a battle on the front lines.

"Don't worry, Mr. Street, I'm not going to shoot you." She paused for a few seconds, then added for effect, "No matter how tempting that thought might be."

"I don't know what kind of scam you're running here, lady, and frankly, I don't care. If you and the guy with the tow truck have something going to bilk anyone crazy enough to drive down that road, you'll have to wait for the next city slicker to pass through."

"Has anyone ever talked to you about your suspicious nature?"

"You'd be a bit gun-shy, too, if some idiot blew up your car."

The color drained from her face. "Someone blew up your car?" she asked incredulously, her eyes wide with shock. "Why?"

"If I knew that, I'd know who put the bomb in my car. I admit the experience has made me somewhat cautious about the sight of guns, knives and objects with fuses. Don't change the subject."

"I haven't lied to you, Mr. Street," she said quietly, having a difficult time shifting away from bombs and blown-up cars. "I am Shay Oakland, and I design the Lady Shay line your sister sells in her stores. I don't hijack strangers for cash or for kicks."

"I'm not buying it," he muttered, shaking his head. "I admit some of the Dream Street designers are a little on the bizarre side, but none of them strap on a six-shooter. Zoe will only wear pink and Inca Charles wears a colonial costume when she makes the bobbin lace she uses in her designs, but they're harmless eccentricities. None of their odd hobbies hurt anyone."

She shrugged her shoulders wearily. "It doesn't matter whether you believe me or not. I don't have time to argue with you. I need to get to Cadance, and you can either come with me to Quincy's in the boat or walk back the way you came."

"If it's money you're after," he persisted, "you're out of luck. I rarely carry cash."

"That's what comes from living in a big city," she said soothingly. "You become suspicious of everything and everyone. I don't want your money, Mr. Street." Her mouth twisted in a rueful grimace. "Money is the least of my problems. Are you coming with me or not?"

"You aren't going anywhere until you explain why you're wearing a gun." His gaze narrowed. He remembered the thought that had occurred to him during the night when he'd heard her pacing the floor. "Are you in some kind of trouble?"

"Not the kind that needs a gun," she answered.

He detected surprise in her voice rather than antagonism, as though she was puzzled by his concern. She wasn't the only one. Dillon was understanding less and less about his reactions to her as the minutes ticked by.

Especially the strange protective possessiveness that had suddenly taken hold.

"Maybe I could help."

"I'm not in any trouble, Mr. Street," she answered, knowing she wasn't being completely honest. Every female chromosome she possessed and a few she hadn't been aware of until now were causing disruptions she could do without.

One of her mother's pearls of wisdom was that a man was the most stubborn creature on earth. According to Shay's multimarried mother, nothing short of dynamite could budge the male of the species when his mind was made up about something. Monica Sutton's suggestion on dealing with men under those conditions was to work around them when it was impossible to work with them. Considering her mother's extensive experience in the field of male development, Shay decided Monica probably knew what she was talking about.

It was time to make a tactical retreat. Shay, feeling a bit dizzy, accidentally stumbled as she took a step away from him. Dillon caught her arm before she fell on her face.

Sliding his arm around her waist to steady her, he said, "You're going to have to pace yourself better than this, Shay. I find it hard to believe Cadance has such an exciting nightlife you can't bear to tear yourself away at a decent hour so you can get some sleep. The shadows under your eyes are a dead giveaway.

You could do with about twenty-four hours' more sleep."

"Why, thank you," Shay murmured. "I just love being told I look like hell. If this is a sample of your techique with women, your reputation is highly overrated."

"I didn't say you look like hell. I was only suggesting you might think about missing a few parties to catch up on your sleep."

The dizziness had passed. "That's me, all right. Party girl."

"With a gun."

She pried his fingers from her waist and stepped to the side, slightly alarmed when she realized how much she had liked leaning on him.

Grabbing the change of subject, she explained, "It's no big mystery. The gun belongs to Quincy."

"The owner of the lake?" When he saw her nod, he asked, "Why does he need a gun?"

The expression in her eyes was as weary as the exhaustion in her voice. "As you've so sweetly pointed out, I've had little sleep in the last thirty-eight hours, and I'm not at my most sociable when I'm tired. To be honest, I get downright cranky. I'm wearing a gun, and to be fair, I should tell you that I know how to use it. Do you really think this is the right moment to give me a hard time?"

"Probably not," he admitted, "but you still haven't convinced me you're not running a scam with the local towing operator." For no other reason except enjoying provoking her into a response, he asked, "How do I know you aren't Bonnie waiting for Clyde to arrive?"

"That does it," she snapped, closing the distance between them. Her fingers closed around his wrist. He had several reasons for allowing her to draw him along with her. If he could get his mind off hoping she was taking him to her bedroom, he might even have been able to think what they were.

On the landing, she shoved open a partially closed door and stood aside. Dillon stepped into the room and looked around. He didn't think this was a good time to tell her that he'd already checked out the workroom yesterday while she was gone. He believed the woman who designed Lady Shay's designs used the workroom. He just wasn't sure this woman was Lady Shay.

A large worktable filled the center of the room, a length of delicate material stretched out on part of the smooth surface. A dressmaker's dummy was standing in front of one of the windows, displaying a nightgown of Swiss batiste trimmed with French lace. A wooden shelf unit was attached to the wall with pegs holding an astonishing supply of thread, mostly cone-shaped spools of white. A smaller table was positioned against one of the walls with a variety of sewing implements neatly arranged and obviously much used. Next to it was an antique rocking chair with padded arms and seat, a tall, standing lamp behind and to one side.

The absence of a sewing machine was more proof this was Lady Shay's workroom than the existence of one would have been. Dream Street used the information that each piece of lingerie in the Lady Shay line was not only an original design but also hand-sewn. A number of customers were willing to pay extra for owning one-of-a-kind.

In case the sight of her workroom hadn't convinced him, Shay held out her left hand several inches from his face. "Look at my fingers, Mr. Street. Those tiny scars are from about a million pin and needle pricks, paper cuts, and the occasional snip of sharp scissors. I'd sit down and whip up a chemise or two for you as additional proof, but I don't have the time."

"I'll concede you are Lady Shay, but you still haven't explained why you're wearing this guy's gun," he persisted.

"As long as the gun isn't pointed at you, I don't see why it should be any of your business."

Dillon stood in front of her with his arms folded across his chest, looking as immovable as a brick wall.

Shay gave him a speculative look, weighing her chances of pushing him any further. She didn't need to know about his past to realize he could be a tough and stubborn opponent. It was there in his eyes and the firm set of his mouth. Fighting with him would be a waste of time. But she found it difficult to back down.

"An elderly man is wandering around alone and confused, and you pick this moment to turn all demanding macho male on me," she said irritably, knowing she was going to lose this minor skirmish.

"I know," he said soothingly. "Men can be such beasts. So what's your answer? Why are you wearing this man's gun?"

She had the feeling Dillon could give a mule lessons in being stubborn. "Quincy is the chief of police of Cadance."

"That explains why he would have a gun, but not what you're doing with it."

"The gun's safety needed to be fixed," she enunciated, measuring the words carefully as though they were heavy. "I had it repaired, and now I'm returning it. I strapped it on because it's easier to wear it than carry it when I'm running a boat." She held her hand in a halting gesture, her palm extended toward him. "I answered your question about the gun, Mr. Street. I showed you proof I am Shay Oakland. If you're about to start in on why I should go to Minneapolis, save your breath. I'm not now, tomorrow, the next day, or any day in the future going to the grand opening of your sister's store. There isn't anything you can say or do to make me change my mind. It's nothing personal. It wouldn't be possible right now even if I wanted to go, which I don't. If you don't come with me now to Quincy's, you'll have a long walk back to town if Travis can't make it out here today. You'd better make up your mind quickly. There's an elderly man with Alzheimer's disease wandering around somewhere, and his wife is waiting for me."

"Phew," he breathed softly. "You have one runaway mouth, sweetheart. Usually I don't go in for chatty women, but I'm going to have to make an exception with you."

"Why, you arrogant..." She glared at him as she searched for just the right word. She would have come up with one, too, if her brain didn't feel as though it was wrapped in cotton. She settled for the only thing she could think of at the moment.

"You dumb jock."

He laughed, which only infuriated her more. She brushed past him and left the room. The leather soles of her shoes hit the wooden stairs rapidly as she hurried down them. It was a miracle she didn't fall, considering her legs felt as strong as cotton candy. She walked quickly into the kitchen. The keys to the boat were hanging on a wooden peg on a wall near the back door. In two seconds she had the keys in one hand and was pushing open the back door with the other.

She'd taken three steps on the crushed-rock path when she realized there were more than her own two feet walking on the gravel. She looked over her shoulder and saw Dillon was only a yard or so behind her. His only response to her glaring look was a single raised brow, as though he was silently questioning her delaying their departure by checking up on him.

Shay couldn't stop the smile from forming on her lips. Her temper had fizzled out as quickly as it had flared. "I wonder how many years I'd get for pushing you out of the boat in the middle of the lake."

"You wouldn't have to be behind bars a single day, angel. I can swim." His long stride had eaten up the space between them, and he passed her as though she was standing still. Glancing at her over his shoulder, he added, "I thought you were in a hurry?"

Shay clenched her teeth and picked up her pace. She wouldn't put it past him to take off in the boat without her!

When they reached the edge of the lake, Dillon examined the boat tied to the left side of a wooden dock that was only about four feet wide. He was no great authority on boats, but this one seemed fairly small and old. Made of highly polished wood, the boat had an inboard motor and was about eighteen feet long. He was encouraged to see the wooden deck was dry. He knew how to swim, but would prefer staying in the boat rather than having to swim from the center of the lake if the boat happened to sink.

Following Shay's instructions, Dillon took the stern line off the dock post after she'd untied the bow line and stepped into the boat. He grabbed one of the dock support posts and climbed aboard. His descent wasn't as graceful as hers had been, but he managed to make the step down without falling into the lake. The height of the dock seemed to him to be exceedingly high in relation to the lake surface. Since he had never been in a boat this small before, he wasn't exactly an expert, so he kept his mouth shut.

He heard the engine roar to life and glanced at the exhaust churning the water behind the boat. Instead of sliding through the opening between the two front seats, he levered a long leg over the bucket seat next to Shay's and sat down on top of the backrest as she had with her feet on the seat. He had barely sat down when Shay hit the throttle and they swept away from the dock.

Dillon figured out that the wind and water spray wouldn't be slapping him in the face if he was sitting down on the seat where the clear windshield would block out both wind and water. Instead he was being blasted by the elements. A glance at Shay showed she didn't appear to mind being battered, bathed and windblown. In fact, she looked as though she was thoroughly enjoying herself.

Sensing his gaze, she took her attention off the lake in front of them and looked at him. "You don't get seasick, do you?"

"Damned if I know. I've never been in a boat quite this tiny before."

"Sorry, we're fresh out of yachts."

He gave her an annoyed glance. "Shouldn't you be looking where you're going?"

Shay managed not to laugh aloud. She recognized a novice when she saw one. "This isn't exactly a six-lane freeway at rush hour. I have the only boat that's out on the lake, and there's nothing between us and Quincy's except water. What would I hit?"

"How the hell would I know?" he muttered, not particularly caring that he sounded cranky. "The way this jaunt to Minnesota has gone so far doesn't give me a lot of confidence in what lies ahead.''

Shay raised her face into the wind as she pushed the throttle down to go faster, closing her eyes briefly as the damp breeze coated her skin. The sun, the water, and the speed of the boat revitalized her almost as much as several additional hours of sleep would have done.

Opening her eyes, she kept her gaze on the water in front of the boat more for Dillon's sake than because it was necessary.

"When do you plan on telling me why you've really come to the wilds of Minnesota, Mr. Street? And don't tell me it's just to persuade me to come to the opening of your sister's store or to remind me I'm late sending in my orders. Mrs. Navarro could have sent any of her staff to do that.''

"She did. Not one of her staff, exactly. A friend of mine is a private investigator. He sent one of his guys out here to check on you when Amy first became concerned when you didn't respond to her letters. Your dogs chased him away.''

"When was this?''

He named the date. It wasn't one he was likely to forget since it was the same day his car was blown into hundreds of high-priced pieces a little over two weeks ago.

"Flynn Tanner was doing me a favor by checking on you for Amy. After Amy contacted your agent and got smoke blown in her face with excuses a sixth grader could make up, she decided she needed personal contact."

"So Mrs. Navarro brought out the big guns and asked you to talk to me?"

"I volunteered."

"A family emergency has kept me occupied. It wouldn't have made a difference even if I had met this detective. I still wouldn't have agreed to go to the grand opening."

"Maybe we should have sent Flynn. He could persuade an icicle to melt in twenty below zero."

"He sounds like a real charmer. You evidently have a lot in common."

"He's my old college roommate. Without his help, I would never have passed physics. Without my help, he wouldn't have made it through English. He was also one hell of a quarterback, but he didn't love the game like I did. After graduation he gave his diploma to his father, who had wanted it more than Flynn did, and took some basic training in the art of surveillance, self-defense and weapons before opening his own office as a private investigator."

"Sending a private investigator here to talk to me is a bit strong, isn't it?" she asked with reproach. "Just because I'm a little late with an order and I turned down the appearance at the grand opening?"

"It was worth a try, but your dogs never gave the investigator a chance to make his pitch."

"So your sister decided to send in the maverick?" She shook her head. "Sorry, I don't buy it. I'm pleased my designs are popular, but I can't supply that many pieces in a year to be the backbone of Dream Street. My attendance at the grand opening can't be that important for you to come halfway across the country just to twist my arm about attending." She grinned suddenly, amusement glittering in her eyes. "And don't try to tell me it's because you wanted to spend a little time in the country. You're having as much fun as a one-legged frog in rush-hour traffic."

"Are you kidding?" Dillon chuckled. "I'm having a great time."

She gave him a skeptical glance just before she cut back the throttle and turned the wheel so the boat was headed toward a dock stretched out over the water from the shoreline. Dillon saw a brief flash of the sun reflecting off glass located among the trees lining the shore. When Shay turned the boat directly toward the dock, Dillon was able to see a sprawling one-story cabin made of aged logs in a clearing between tall fir trees.

Dillon was puzzled by a stretch of raw wood construction built on a slant from a sprawling wooden deck. The width of the ramp was wide enough for two people to walk comfortably side-by-side. The newness of the boards was a sharp contrast to the weathered condition of the rest of the cabin. A separate building with a wide opening facing the lake was positioned so that it hung over a portion of the water. The wide door was closed so Dillon couldn't see in the shed, but he made a wild guess that it was a boat-house.

He put his hand out to brace himself on the top edge of the windshield when Shay cut the throttle completely. They coasted slowly toward one side of the dock. Before he even thought about it, Shay was out of the boat and had tied a boat hitch several times over one of the pilings. She had just finished securing the stern line when he levered himself onto the dock.

Instead of charging past him as he'd expected, Shay stopped in front of him, a teasing smile curving her mouth. "Now, that wasn't so bad, was it?"

An almost uncontrollable surge of desire made his stomach muscles clench. Her voice was as soft as a cloud, her smile as intoxicating as a sip of expensive Scotch. He resisted stroking her cheek where sunlight warmed her skin. It wasn't easy.

"It was a thrill a minute." He fell into step beside her when she began walking toward the cabin. "Exactly what is your relationship with this Quincy guy? You evidently know him fairly well if you and he share a private lake, and you pop in and out without calling ahead."

"It's a little complicated. I suppose the easiest explanation is, he's my father."

"Your father? This Quincy guy is your father?"

"You'll have to take my word for it."

"How is that complicated? Aside from the fact that you have two different last names, the relationship is fairly common. A lot of people have fathers."

"So I've heard," she said, without going into details of how her relationship with Quincy was different from the norm. Her illegitimacy wasn't something she usually talked about after a long acquaintance, much less to a complete stranger. She had worked for Dream Street for several years and knew quite a bit about Amy Navarro's background, and had known about Dillon Street through conversations with her father and through what she'd read in magazines and newspapers. The man himself was still an unknown factor. She had no idea what his reaction to her birth status would be. It didn't matter. It was none of his business.

Dillon saw the closed look on her face. Each answer from her so far had only created more curiosity and further questions in his mind.

Walking up the grassy incline toward the house, Dillon could see there were wooden steps under the ramp that were as weathered as the gray logs of the cabin. Apparently the need for the ramp addition was only recent.

Shay stepped up onto the slanted walkway and approached the sliding-glass door situated between two wide windows. With her hand on the latch, she turned to Dillon, her expression guarded. "I suppose I should warn you that Quincy has not been in the best of moods since he was injured in a car accident. Most of the time his bark is worse than his bite," she said. "But if he's had a bad night, he can come close to verbally ripping off a layer of skin. We had a serious argument two nights ago, so I'm not sure what his mood will be this morning when he sees me. If he is willing, I'm going to leave you here with him while I look for Mr. Varanger. I'll contact Travis again before I leave and ask him to pick you up here before he goes after your car. It'll be out of his way, but you'll be able to go into town with him when he tows your car. That way you won't be stranded here too long."

Dillon reached across her and put his hand over hers on the latch and turned it. When he released the latch, he brought her hand away with his.

"I'm a big boy now, Shay. You don't need to worry about me. Go do what you have to do to find the elderly man, and I'll take care of getting the car out of your lane."

She looked doubtful, but Dillon didn't press. He even released her hand when she tried to pull her fingers free. She had no idea how unusual it was for him to be so cooperative. When he wanted something, he normally went after it with little regard as to whether it suited anyone else or not. He'd never realized that until now.

Stepping into the cabin, Shay called out, "Quincy? It's me, Shay."

The sound of rubber wheels on the wood plank floor was heard before a man's gruff voice growled, "And who else would it be?"

Shay breathed a sigh of relief when she heard the hint of tolerant amusement in his gruff voice. He had been sullen and silent when she'd left his cabin after their heated argument. They'd both said some things they shouldn't have, delved into the past that they usually left alone. The strain of coping with the abrupt changes in Quincy's life had finally taken its toll on both of them in the defenseless dark hours that night.

Quincy had been rude to most of the visitors who had come to see him after the accident, and those people were friends he'd known for many years. Maybe Dillon Street would come off lightly because of who he was, she hoped. Quincy was a fanatical football fan.

Dillon stood quietly beside her as they waited for Quincy to maneuver the wheelchair down the hallway from his bedroom. Shay jerked her head around to look at the man standing beside her when she felt Dillon's hand at the back of her neck, his thumb stroking the taut muscles caused by tension she wasn't aware she was feeling until that moment. She couldn't read his expression as he met her puzzled gaze. She broke eye contact first.

When Shay saw Quincy's moccasins on the footrest of the wheelchair appear, she stepped away from Dillon's disturbing touch. She had enough explanations to make without adding why Dillon Street was touching her as though it was his right. Since she didn't understand why Dillon felt she needed his silent support, she certainly couldn't explain it to Quincy.

With two strokes of his powerful arms, her father propelled the wheelchair into the spacious living room.

The older man's large frame was covered in a faded, shapeless, light gray plaid flannel robe with navy blue cotton pajamas underneath. She was heartily sick of his choice of clothing, but any attempt to persuade him to get dressed had met with stubborn resistance. Quincy McCall was a barrel-chested man with light blue eyes that could drill into a man with the intensity of a laser. His skin was tanned and creased by age, sunshine, and a once active outdoor life.

"I'm not able to walk, Shay, but my hearing is fine." He frowned darkly when he saw the man beside her. Shay and Dillon were standing with their backs to the windows, their faces in shadow. "Who the hell is this?"

"This is Dillon Street. He's managed to get his car stuck in my lane. I'm going to call Travis to have him bring out his tow truck so Mr. Street can be on his way. Mr. Street, this is Quincy McCall."

Dillon took the two steps necessary to bring him up to the wheelchair. Extending his right hand, he ignored the older man's scowl and said, "I'm pleased to meet you." He glanced at Quincy's robe and pajamas. "I'm sorry if we disturbed your rest."

Shay closed her eyes briefly as she waited for the explosion. Dillon had made a natural assumption but an inaccurate one. Quincy hadn't bothered getting dressed since his accident, which meant he'd lived in pajamas night and day for two months.

After a few seconds she raised her lashes when Dillon's apology was met with only silence and not a colorful explosion of curse words. She was surprised to see a gleam of interest in Quincy's light blue eyes as he stared up at Dillon. It seemed like forever since she'd seen any expressions on his face other than irritation, fury, frustration and pain.

Leaning forward after shaking Dillon's hand briefly, Quincy rested his forearms on the sides of the chair and studied the tall man beside Shay. "I'll be damned," he murmured. "The Maverick in Minnesota. You're one hell of a wide receiver, Mr. Street."

"Was. I'm retired, but thanks. And it's Dillon, not Mr. Street." Dillon's gaze shifted to Shay unhooking the gun holster from her belt. He wondered if he was imagining the tension between father and daughter. "But I guess being a football player is like being a policeman. Even if we are no longer active, it's still part of who we are."

A variety of expressions crossed Quincy's face as he considered what Dillon had said. To Shay's amazement, Quincy was weighing the younger man's words carefully, rather than lashing him with his temper as he had Shay when she'd said basically the same thing only in different words.

She nearly dropped the revolver when Quincy said with a degree of warmth, "A football player and a philosopher. That's an unusual combination, Maverick. If you've got the time, maybe you could fill me in on a few things I've often wondered about professional football."

"A lot has changed since I played professionally. You've probably experienced something similar in police work. Procedures change. Rules are added and eliminated. Nothing ever stays the same."

Quincy's unshaven face held a look of disgust. "Tell me about it. When I was a rookie, we..."

Shay tuned out the story she'd heard many times before. Bemused by the events of the past few minutes, she watched Dillon step around to the back of the wheelchair and push it toward a grouping of easy chairs and sofa while Quincy continued telling Dillon about his early days on the force. Dillon positioned Quincy so the older man would be facing the chair he sat down in. They began to discuss new football rules and regulations versus old ones.

Feeling as though she had suddenly become invisible, Shay walked over to a rolltop desk and slid back the curved front. It took her only a few seconds to slip the holster into the cubbyhole where, for as long as Shay could remember, Quincy had kept his revolver when he was off duty. She hoped she was doing the right thing by bringing the gun back. Quincy still had a long way to go toward adjusting to his physical restrictions, but she felt he wasn't as depressed as he'd been for weeks after the accident. Oddly enough, the heated argument they'd had the other night had given her the first real hope that Quincy was adjusting to his disability. He'd argued that she was treating him like a helpless baby instead of a man. Bringing his gun back was her way to show him she believed he wouldn't give in to the urge to end his life.

She felt her father's gaze on her and looked up. He glanced at the holstered gun, then nodded once abruptly before turning his attention back to Dillon.

She closed the rolltop and went to the phone, which happened to be on the small table next to the chair Dillon had taken. The two men were engrossed in a deep philosophical discussion on the pros and cons of artificial turf and didn't look her way when she approached. She picked up the receiver, moved away as far as the extra-long cord would stretch, and punched in the phone number she'd used last night. Her fingers played with the cord as she waited for someone at Travis's Garage to answer.

She almost gasped when she heard Quincy chuckling. It was a sound she thought she would never hear again. Turning around, she saw Dillon was standing several feet away from Quincy's chair, his right arm flung back as though he was about to throw a ball. Then Dillon tripped over his own foot while describing the excuse the quarterback gave later in the locker room. Quincy was hanging on every word, a look of complete absorption on his face, a drastic change from the petulant frown Shay had been confronting the past two months.

She shook her head in bemusement. Of all the things she'd tried in an effort to bring her father out of his depression since the accident, she never once thought of bringing him someone to play with!

The number she'd called was finally answered on the eleventh ring, and she relayed the problem with Dillon's car to Travis Trotter, the owner and operator of the only automotive repair business within twenty miles. She frowned when he stated he couldn't come until the next morning. The mayor's car was on the blink again, and His Honor needed it to show a couple of out-of-town businessmen around town to talk them into bringing their car dealership to Cadance. Shay cut Travis off before he could get started on his opinion of whether or not the town really needed a car franchise. Travis always had opinions about something or other, and she had a few other priorities.

Like what she was going to do with Dillon Street until tomorrow. Cadance had one motel that was still recovering from a rainstorm that had dumped too much water on its flat roof, the weight of the accumulated water collapsing the ceilings of nine of the ten units.

"What about your cousin who took over the station while you took Opal and the kids to Graceland?" she asked hopefully. "Mr. Street doesn't want to stick around any longer than necessary."

She thought Dillon was occupied with his conversation with her father, but he turned his head and gave her a dark look. She lifted her chin and stared back, refusing to be intimidated.

Her suggestion was shot down by Travis. "Norris is putting in overtime at the cement plant." She heard him sigh heavily before adding, "I'll try to get out there today if I can. That's all I can promise."

"Thanks, Travis. If you can make it today, could you pick up Mr. Street at Quincy's before you go to my place?"

Hanging up the phone after Travis grudgingly agreed to her last request, Shay replaced it on the table and waited for a break in the conversation to tell Quincy she was leaving and why. She had a long wait.

Thoughts of Mrs. Varanger waiting for her made her eventually clear her throat to interrupt, and both men looked up at her with similar expressions of surprise. "Gee, you guys are great for a girl's ego." She didn't give them an opportunity to respond. "Jewel said she called you about Mr. Varanger, Quincy."

He scowled. "Of course she did. I'm still chief of police. I told her to send Brad out to check with the neighbors." He tapped his watch with his forefinger. "Jewel called over an hour ago and I'm sure she obeyed my instructions to notify you right away. We made an agreement, Shay. Why aren't you on your way to the Varangers'?"

"I've gone out on every call since your accident, Quincy, just as I promised I would," she answered, uncomfortably aware of the warm embarrassed flush on her cheeks at his accusing tone.

"On my orders only. That doesn't mean you can take over completely as you have here. I'm still the chief of police until June first. I give the orders and you help Brad and Yale in the field. That was our deal.''

Her stomach tightened with tension. "I haven't forgotten. I'm also not a robot, Quincy. I don't operate on motor oil, and you can't push my buttons night and day to make me perform for you." She lifted her hands and dropped them again in a defeated gesture. "Never mind. Forget it. We went over all this the other night. It's a waste of time and as you've just reminded me, I have work to do in town. While I'm gone, do you mind if Mr. Street stays here until I can figure out what to do with him?"

Dillon bristled. "You make me sound as though I'm some nasty lump of manure that's been left on your doorstep. Mr. McCall and—"

"Quincy," interjected her father.

Dillon nodded in the older man's direction, silently agreeing to the first-name basis. "Quincy and I will be fine here." He had another thought. "Unless you could use my help looking for the missing man."

"I'm hoping it won't take long to find Mr. Varanger, but thanks for the offer." She told Quincy what she planned to do and asked if he could think of anything else they should be doing. He gave a couple of suggestions which she agreed to before she turned to Dillon. "Travis is going to try to tow your car today, but he can't guarantee he can make it. While I'm in town, I'll stop at the Cadance Motel and see if they have a vacancy for tonight."

Quincy protested, "He can't stay there, Shay. You told me the motel has plastic stretched over the roof."

"When I checked out their damage after the storm, Nina said one of the units was reasonably habitable. If it is unoccupied, I'll book it for Mr. Street."

Dillon didn't waste his breath arguing. Shay could make all the reservations she wanted. That didn't mean he had to use them. His accommodations last night weren't perfect, but better than an impersonal motel. And close to Shay.

Shay was standing only a foot away from Quincy, yet Dillon detected a distance in her voice.

"Did you have any breakfast this morning?"

"Yes, Mommy," her father replied sarcastically. "I ate all my pablum like a good boy."

"Quincy..."

He held up a hand, his tone cutting and sharp. "I meant what I said the other night, Shay. I'm not a child, and you have to stop treating me like one. If you want a child, get married and have your own."

Shay refused to go over their argument in front of an audience. "If you know how I can take care of you, your house, and your job without hurting your feelings, let me know, Quincy. In the meantime, stop hurting mine. I'm doing the best I can."

She walked away, her back straight and so tense Dillon wouldn't have been surprised if her spine snapped in two. He followed her after telling Quincy he would be back in a moment.

He caught up with Shay when she stopped at the end of one of the cupboards in the kitchen, where a series of nails were used as a receptacle for key rings. He knew she was aware of him even though her back was to him. As soon as he'd walked into the kitchen, she'd stiffened her spine even more, although he didn't see how that was possible. Her fingers hesitated a few seconds before closing around the keys. He saw her knuckles turn white with the force of her grip. She reminded him of a wire stretched dangerously tight to the point of breaking.

Dillon stopped only inches from her and lifted the thick braid lying against her jacket. He gave it a gentle tug when she didn't look at him. The keys jangled as she turned to face him. He saw she had used the short time to shore up her defenses.

"Are you all right?" he asked quietly.

"Of course," she answered.

"Of course," he repeated with a faint smile. He had the feeling she wouldn't admit it if she had a hundred and three temperature. This wasn't the first time he had gotten the impression she had been blessed with a sizable chunk of stubborn pride. He had a healthy share of pride, too, and was irritated that she was shutting him out.

"Would you like to tell me what that was all about?"

"No," she said flatly. "Have you changed your mind about staying here?" she asked. "Even if you go to town with me, I can't guarantee Travis can get to your car any faster.''

He shook his head, his gaze serious and searching. ''I'll keep your father company until you get back. It would help if I knew what topics to avoid, like whether or not he wants to talk about his injury. After my knee operation, I wasn't exactly the sweetest guy in San Francisco. I didn't want to discuss my operation, my career, even the weather with anyone. I was too busy feeling sorry for myself. Like Quincy, I didn't get dressed until about the fourth day after being released from the hospital when I couldn't stand myself any longer.''

''Quincy's accident was two months ago,'' she informed him. ''He hasn't worn anything except pajamas and a robe since. Only under threat of my taking a razor to him myself does he eventually bathe and shave.''

Dillon was so surprised by her answer, he released her braid and stared at her. ''I took it for granted he was only temporarily out of commission.''

''He was chasing a couple of teenagers one night who'd 'borrowed' a car without permission. There's an S curve outside of town toward Stafford Junction that is too dangerous to navigate over twenty-five miles per hour. Three months before the accident, the highway department had put up a warning sign. The teenagers made it going fifty. Quincy didn't make it at all. He injured his lower spine when his car went off the road. The prognosis is he'll never be able to walk again.''

Dillon listened to the explanation of the older man's injury. He realized Shay wasn't going into how the accident had affected her life, but Dillon's imagination could fill in the blanks. The strain and exhaustion in her eyes and the reason for her delay in filling the lingerie order for Dream Street were explained.

He stroked the back of a knuckle under one of her eyes. ''Is two months of worrying and taking care of your father responsible for these purple shadows under your eyes?''

Shay stepped away from him so he was no longer touching her. She liked the feel of his hands on her too much. It would be so easy to respond to the gentleness in his voice, to the tenderness in his touch. But incredibly stupid. He made her feel both weak and strong at a time when she was neither. Just tired. So damn tired.

''I appreciate your staying here with him.'' She rubbed her fingers across her forehead, but the action didn't erase the headache beginning to throb in her temples. ''He's enjoying your company. Today was the first time I've heard him laugh since the accident. While I'm in town, I'll see if I can talk Travis into working a little later today, so you won't have to stick around any longer than is necessary.''

Dillon had found the procedure used in football of charging ahead no matter what obstacle stood in his path often worked in real-life situations, as well.

"Have you had any help in taking care of your father during the last two months?"

She shook her head. "Quincy is a very proud man. He doesn't want anyone to know just how seriously he's been injured. Being chief of police has been his whole life. Losing his job on top of his disability is a lot to accept. At least he's getting his fighting spirit back, even though I'm the one he's fighting at the moment."

"Why are you going out on police calls? Because of the agreement you made after the accident?"

"That's part of it. This is a small town where everyone knows everyone else. They trust Quincy. Because I'm his daughter, they trust me, too. But they like to think he's still in charge. His two deputies are too young and inexperienced. It took two years of taking pre-law before I decided I wasn't tough enough to be a lawyer. But I'm familiar with the law and state and city codes. I've been sworn in as a deputy to make it all legal. This is not a high-crime area and so far nothing's come up I can't handle."

There wasn't much Dillon could do to ease her burden except carry a little of the load on his shoulders for a while.

"How about if I stay with your father tonight? All night. That way you can get some sleep and not have to worry about him, and I won't have to stare at a plastic ceiling at the motel all night."

"I can't let you do that," she said emphatically. "Quincy is my responsibility, not yours. If I can persuade Travis to come out for your car today, you can be on your way back to San Francisco by tonight.''

What he was about to say wasn't going to thrill her. "I wasn't going to break this to you until later, since you have enough on your mind, but you might as well know now so you can get it out of your system while you're gone. I'm not going to return to San Francisco after Travis gets the car out of the lane.''

She made an exasperated sound deep in her throat. "I don't know how else I can convince you that I'm not going to be attending the grand opening no matter what you say or do.''

He grinned as he gently pushed her toward the back door. "I might have lost a little yardage, but I can still make a touchdown.''

She glanced at him over her shoulder. "What does that mean?''

He lowered his head and touched his mouth briefly to hers. "It means you're in big trouble, sweetheart.''

Chapter Five

When she stared at him, he met her gaze without smiling. She couldn't have looked more stunned if he'd stripped off all his clothes.

"You're crazy," she murmured softly.

"Not yet, but I can't promise how long I'll be sane if I don't kiss you soon."

"You just did."

A corner of his mouth curved into a sensual smile. "No, Lady Shay. I mean a real kiss—deep, hard, and hot."

Shay turned away abruptly, missing the last step in her haste to put some distance between them. Dillon murmured a soft curse and grabbed her arm as her left foot landed awkwardly on the ground.

"That does it!" he growled. He pulled her back to the steps. "Stay there," he ordered as he forced her to sit down on the middle step.

"I don't have time for any more of your games," she protested.

"You don't have any sense. That's the problem. You also don't have a choice. Wait here until I come back."

She glared at him. "You don't own me. I'll go where I want, when I want."

He leaned forward until his face was only inches away from hers. "Don't make the mistake of thinking I'm all talk and no action, Shay. Stay where you are until I get back."

She wished she could summon up enough anger to give her the strength to disobey him and suffer the consequences. It didn't matter. He didn't give her the opportunity to object even if she could have whipped up something to say. Dillon climbed the steps two at a time and disappeared into Quincy's cabin.

Shay propped her elbows on her knees and buried her face in her hands while she waited for the dizziness to pass. A few seconds later she heard the murmur of voices. Breathing deeply, she gradually felt less light-headed, although the headache was swiftly moving up the pain scale to a ten.

When she thought she could possibly walk without falling on her face, she stood.

She'd taken two fairly steady steps toward her truck when she heard Dillon's voice behind her. "Where do you think you're going?"

"To look for Mr. Varanger." She turned her head to look at him a little too quickly. Hoping her head would stay attached, she chided, "Pay attention, will you, Street? Remember the call from the dispatcher? It's why we left my cabin."

"You aren't going to help the Varangers or anyone else if you pass out behind the wheel and end up in a ditch."

"I was a little dizzy for a few seconds," she protested as she yanked open the door on the driver's side of the truck. "Don't make such a big deal out of it."

It required more effort than it should have for her to hoist herself up to the seat behind the wheel. She was reaching for the safety belt when the passenger door was suddenly yanked open and Dillon climbed in.

"Where do you think you're going?"

"I don't think. I know," he said in a tone that dared her to argue with him. "I told Quincy I was going with you."

"Why?"

He reached over and turned the key in the ignition when she didn't. "Try to stay out of the ditches along the road. I dislike hospitals."

Between the pain in her head and exhaustion sapping her strength, she didn't have the energy to push him out of the truck, although the idea was very tempting.

As she drove, she turned on the radio to discourage conversation. After a few seconds of throbbing guitars and beating drums, she quickly turned it off when the rock music clashed with the cymbals clanging in her temples. She settled for rolling down a window to let fresh air in. She was thankful that Dillon remained silent. The simple act of driving the truck was requiring all her concentration.

Shay blinked several times to clear her vision when the smooth paved road suddenly became rough under the tires. She had driven onto the shoulder of the paved road with all the finesse of a novice driver. She turned the steering wheel to bring the truck back onto the pavement.

The caustic comment she expected from Dillon never came. Not a single word. When Shay glanced in his direction, he was looking straight ahead, his lips pursed as he softly whistled a tune under his breath.

Four minutes later she drove off the road again, this time on purpose. Shay opened the door, slid down to the ground, walked around the front of the truck, and opened the passenger door.

"You drive."

All he did was nod curtly and swing his legs over to the ground. It was a perfect opportunity for him to gloat, and Shay was pleasantly surprised when he refrained. She sank down onto the seat he'd vacated and closed her eyes against the sun coming through the windshield. The bright light sent shards of sharp pain through her head, making her wish she'd remembered to bring her sunglasses. She heard Dillon shut the door and waited for him to put the truck in gear.

When she felt his forearm brush against her breast, she opened her eyes and found him leaning over her.

"What are you doing?" she asked with indignation as she attempted to push his arm away.

"Relax, sweetheart," he drawled. "I'm only hooking up your seat belt." He pulled the straps across her and clicked the belt into place. "When I make a pass, you won't have to ask what I'm doing."

"If," she murmured.

"When," he countered.

Shay shut her eyes again. Changing the subject seemed a wise thing to do. "Keep on this road until you get to a three-story brick building on the corner with swings and slides behind it."

"You can say school. I'll know what it is, Shay. We even have them in big cities."

"Turn right at the school," she murmured, emphasizing the last word. "Go four blocks, turn left, then another right turn. The Varangers live in the third house on the left." She scowled, her eyes still closed. "Or is it the second house?"

Her sleepy drawl was causing odd rushes of heat along his veins. Damn, he cursed silently. Everything she did made him think of sex. His arm was still tingling from the brief contact with her breast even through the sleeve of his jacket. He wondered if she sounded that seductive after she made love. Or during. Or before.

This time it was his turn to nearly go into the ditch.

Shay opened her eyes to glance in his direction when she was thrown against the straps of the seat belt as he turned the wheel sharply to return to the lane he was supposed to be in. Then he looked at her briefly, his dark eyes daring her to make a remark about his driving.

All she said was "I was right the first time. It's the third house on the left."

Arriving at the white clapboard house that had been in the Varanger family for three generations, Shay asked Dillon to park behind the patrol car that was in the driveway. She glanced down the street and saw the young deputy was ringing the doorbell of a house halfway down the block.

Shay took a deep breath and climbed down from the truck. She wasn't looking forward to this. Emma Varanger had at one time been a cheerful woman who'd always had cookies and milk on hand when any of the neighborhood children stopped by after school. Shay had occasionally taken advantage of Mrs. Varanger's hospitality when she'd been in school even though their house hadn't been on her normal route home.

Time and circumstances had taken their toll on the elderly couple, and Shay wished life hadn't become so difficult for them at this stage of their lives.

Thinking of her mother suddenly, Shay had to admit life could hand out a number of surprises to people; some they'd asked for without realizing it and others they hadn't wanted.

As Shay walked up the driveway, she passed a four-foot, gray stone wall that separated the Varangers from their neighbors on one side. "I used to lean my bicycle against that wall after school. Then I'd go into the screened-in porch where Mrs. Varanger served milk and homemade cookies to every child who appeared at her door."

Dillon glanced at the stone wall and tried to visualize a smaller, younger version of Shay Oakland. His imagination was usually above average but picturing Shay as anything other than the adult sensuous woman in front of him wasn't possible.

Shay opened the door to the back porch and walked in. The circular table sitting in the middle of four café-style chairs was bare today, as it had been for the last two years. There were no crocheted doily centerpieces, plates of fragrant warm cookies, or pitchers of creamy milk. Instead of children's chatter and Mrs. Varanger's softly spoken questions about their day at school, the porch was silent and bare.

Before Shay could rap on the door leading into the kitchen, it was opened, and a petite woman who barely came up to Shay's shoulders managed a warm smile.

"I'm so glad you could come, Shay."

"I wish it was under other circumstances, Mrs. Varanger."

The elderly woman raised her hand and moved it back and forth several times as though she was erasing a blackboard. "You're here now. That's what's important."

Mrs. Varanger stood aside and invited her in. Then the older woman saw Dillon.

Shay introduced him. "This is Dillon Street, Mrs. Varanger. He's visiting from out of town and has volunteered to help us search for Mr. Varanger."

Emma Varanger held out a frail hand and gave Dillon a shy smile. "How kind of you, Mr. Street."

Dillon clasped the elderly woman's hand gently. It was like holding a frail butterfly, easily crushed by a heavy hand. "It's a pleasure to meet you."

The older woman smiled. "Thank you. Please come in."

Shay stepped inside, followed by Dillon, who closed the door quietly behind him. She tried to keep the concern out of her voice when she glanced down at the fragile woman in front of her. Mrs. Varanger was wearing a gray cotton dress with a lace collar and tiny pearl buttons down the front. Her usually tidy, blue-white hair was escaping from the rolled bun at the nape of her neck. Each time Shay saw Emma Varanger, she seemed more fragile and worn down by the heavy responsibility of caring for her husband of forty years.

She looked up at Shay with dull eyes that were haunted with worry. "How is Quincy today?"

Even frantic about her husband, the distraught woman thought of someone else's problems, thought Shay. She put her arm around Mrs. Varanger's thin shoulders and drew her toward the front room the small woman always referred to as the parlor.

"He's doing much better, Mrs. Varanger. He appreciated the date cookies you sent over last week."

Her voice thick with tears too near the surface, the elderly woman said, "It's so hard to understand how once-strong men can be brought down by circumstances they can't control. It seems so cruel."

Shay directed Mrs. Varanger to a platform rocker in the living room and gently pressed her to sit down. She saw the other woman glance toward the empty upholstered chair where her husband usually sat. A heartfelt sigh filled the silence in the room.

"We'll find Mr. Varanger soon, Mrs. Varanger," Shay said soothingly, hoping she was telling the truth. "How long has it been since you last saw him?"

Mrs. Varanger glanced at the Black Forest cuckoo clock on the wall. "It was a few minutes before nine when I came in here to check on him. I had been in the kitchen checking on a pot of chicken vegetable soup I was making for his lunch. I try to keep meals to a regular schedule, although..." Her voice trailed off into silence.

Shay didn't need to ask the elderly woman what she'd been about to say. Mrs. Varanger was keeping to a schedule mainly for herself. Mr. Varanger had no concept of time.

"What was he wearing when you last saw him? I know you've told Quincy's deputy, but now I need you to tell me."

"He was wearing gray cotton slacks and shirt, but as I told Bradley, your father's deputy, Arnold might have taken them off." She slid an embarrassed glance in Dillon's direction. "My husband has become quite erratic lately due to his illness. He's not himself."

Dillon smiled faintly. "I don't shock easily, Mrs. Varanger. The main thing is to find him."

As much as she would like to stay to comfort the elderly woman, Shay wanted to start looking for Emma's husband as soon as possible.

"Could I get you a cup of tea before I leave, or call someone to stay with you?"

The older woman shook her head. "No. Thank you, dear. I'd rather you look for Arnold. I can't bear the thought of him out there somewhere, frightened and alone and not understanding what was happening."

Shay laid her hand over Mrs. Varanger's cold, clenched fingers in her lap. "We'll find him, Mrs. Varanger. I know it's difficult, but try to relax."

The older woman's hand was remarkably strong when she suddenly gripped Shay's. "He's taken the shotgun this time, Shay. He's never done that before. I'm afraid he's going to hurt himself or someone else."

Shay bent down in front of Mrs. Varanger's chair. "Dr. Pritchard told you that Mr. Varanger was often living in another time. He used to walk his dog in

Ryerson Woods. That's the first place I'm going to look."

"Do be careful, child. Arnold wouldn't normally hurt you for all the world, but..."

Shay nodded her understanding and gave the older woman's clasped hands a gentle pat before straightening.

"I'll be back with Mr. Varanger as soon as possible," she stated, hoping she was once again telling the truth. "Why don't you fix some of your wonderful dumplings to go with your chicken soup? He's going to be pretty hungry when we bring him back."

They both knew Arnold couldn't remember when his last meal had been, but the task would give Mrs. Varanger something to do to fill the time she had to wait for her husband's return.

Shay waited by the door while Dillon said goodbye, impressed with the gentle kindness he was giving to the elderly woman. Shay didn't want to see Dillon Street's sensitive nature. She could resist his arrogance. Discovering he could be tender and sympathetic weakened her resolve to fight the attraction between them.

Her thoughts ran ahead to what she had to do next. Brad evidently wasn't having any luck with the neighbors or he would have been back by now with either a report or the elderly man himself. She would tell the deputy where she was going, but in case her hunch was wrong, he should continue his house-to-house search.

When Dillon joined her at the door, they left Mrs. Varanger's house. The toe of Shay's shoe caught on a crack in the walkway at the bottom of the stairs, and she would have fallen if Dillon hadn't caught her in time. His grip was tight, but not hard enough to hurt her. She was tempted to sag against him, just for a few minutes. She'd depended on herself most of her life, but she would like to have someone to lean on for a little while.

She took a deep breath, irritated with herself when she heard the ragged tension in her breathing. She pushed away from Dillon and said, "Now you know why I never took ballet class."

His brown eyes narrowed in anger, his automatic response to her obvious exhaustion. It was better than letting her see how concerned he was. "Damn it, Shay! You're almost dead on your feet."

"Not quite," she murmured. "You might find this hard to believe, but I'm usually not this clumsy. My feet don't seem to want to go where I tell them to when I'm tired."

"That's because your brain isn't functioning any better than the rest of you. If it was, you'd be in bed getting some sleep."

"What a lovely thought," she murmured dreamily. Responsibility was crowded out briefly by the pleasure of thinking about closing her eyes and giving in to the drugging exhaustion sapping her strength.

"Isn't there anyone else who can look for Mr. Varanger?" he asked.

"Quincy doesn't want this to turn into a circus. Some of our concerned citizens can get carried away, and Mrs. Varanger would be embarrassed by a lot of curious, well-meaning people hovering over her. If we haven't found him in a couple of hours, I'll ask the voluntary fire department to help." She pulled away from him and took a deep, restoring breath. "I need to talk to Quincy's deputy. He's just down the street. I'll tell him where I'm going so we don't duplicate efforts."

"Damn it, Shay." Dillon felt an unfamiliar helplessness, torn between the beseeching look in Mrs. Varanger's eyes and the exhaustion in Shay's. "I don't know what the problem is between you and your father, but you don't need to kill yourself to prove anything to him or to yourself."

Shay placed her hand on his chest, not to push him away but simply to make contact. "I'm not doing this because of my promise to Quincy, Dillon. The Varangers have been kind to me and to just about everyone else in town. It wouldn't be right to abandon them when they need help."

"You are a lingerie designer, Shay, not a cop. I understand why you want to help Mrs. Varanger find her husband, but I also see an exhausted woman who has about used up all her reserves and is operating on sheer stubbornness."

She let her hand drop and turned toward the truck. "I'll rest after we find Mr. Varanger."

Dillon fell into step beside her. Since he couldn't stop her short of handcuffing her to a bed, he shifted his priorities to finding the elderly man. "Would any neighbors take Mr. Varanger inside their home if they found him wandering around?"

"Most of the people in town know Arnold and his situation and would have called the police station, his wife, or the medical clinic if they had seen him out wandering around."

"I still don't understand why you won't ask for more help from the fire department now rather than wait."

"Mr. Varanger broke a hip last year and has severe arthritis. He can't walk very fast or very far. The last time he wandered off, we found him in a garage just down the street. If we haven't located him by four o'clock, I'll contact the volunteer fire department. I don't want Mr. Varanger to spend the night on his own."

"This Ryerson Woods you mentioned to Mrs. Varanger, is it far? Could he have made it to those woods in the time he's been gone?"

"I don't know. The woods start about two blocks from here. It used to be one of his favorite places when they had a dog, so I thought I'd look for him there first. Sometimes Mr. Varanger's mind slips back to the past, to times when he was happy. It's just a hunch, but as good a place to look as any other."

Dillon started to reach for the latch to open the door for Shay when he heard a short, abrupt, loud bang from close by. He wrapped one arm around Shay's waist, one hand tucking her face into his neck, and clamped her to him as he made a rolling dive onto the grass from the driveway to the stone wall. The only protection he could provide for Shay was his body and the wall, which was better than being in the open. He cursed himself for forgetting to be cautious and for putting Shay in danger. He realized he'd dropped his guard shortly after meeting Shay, a real stupid and possibly fatal thing to do.

The shot wasn't repeated. His enemy was either settling for the one attempt or waiting for him to show himself to get a better aim.

Or perhaps he was moving in closer.

Damn, he hated this helplessness. Dodging bullets was completely different from blocking two hundred pounds of animosity on a football field. He would have taken a chance and made a run for the truck if he'd been alone. But he couldn't take the risk of Shay getting in the way of a bullet aimed at him.

Instead of hearing another crack of a gun being fired, Dillon heard the muffled sound of someone gasping for air. He raised up onto his forearms and looked down at the woman under him. Shay's lips were parted as she tried to pull air into her lungs. He realized he had knocked the wind out of her.

He eased his weight off her chest to make it easier for her to breathe. The change in position brought his lower body into the cradle of her hips, which hadn't been his intention at all. He sucked in his breath.

Thoughts of gunshots, exploding cars and death threats faded for a moment as he felt how perfectly their bodies fitted together. He was lying between her legs, and he couldn't do a damn thing to control his body's reaction to the intimate position.

Since he had no way of knowing if there would be another shot or not, Dillon eased his weight off her by rolling partially onto his side so Shay was between him and the wall. He kept one arm under her and laid his other hand just below her breasts. She was still breathing fast, too fast.

"Take it easy, Shay," he said soothingly. "You had the wind knocked out of you. Try to breathe slowly and deeply."

Her gaze never left his face as she followed his instruction. Once she could breathe normally again, she became aware of Dillon Street's hard body pressed against hers. And very conscious of his body's reaction to their intimate position.

She could also feel he was as tense as a coiled spring. Since she had no idea what had set him off, Shay had no way of knowing how violent his response would be to anything she might say or do. Yet they couldn't very well stay where they were indefinitely like an X-rated lawn ornament.

The scent of his skin and the heat from his body were creating a major debate within her as to which was the more potent. Oddly enough, she wasn't frightened by his bizarre action. She was puzzled, but for some odd reason, she knew he wouldn't hurt her.

Maybe football players suffered from flashbacks like military veterans, she speculated with wry amusement.

"Was it something I said?" she asked cautiously.

Dillon saw the hint of humor in her eyes and the knotted tension in his chest loosened. "Are you all right?"

"Now that my lungs are working again, I'm fine. How about you?"

"Check back with me once we're safely away from here."

She became aware of his weight pressing her into something small and hard under her left hip. In an effort to ease the discomfort, she raised her lower body and shifted away from the object digging into her, inadvertently rubbing against him. She heard him suck in his breath and met his gaze. His dark eyes were gleaming with an intensity that sent the blood pounding in her veins like hot lava. Their intimate position created a fire storm of sensations that made her ache to press into his aroused body again and again in an attempt to ease the coiled tension in her body.

"I have a problem," he murmured.

"I know," she breathed. She could feel him hard and hot against her hip.

A corner of his mouth curved upward. "That's not what I meant. We can't stay here forever, but I don't want to move away from you. That's my problem."

"This could get embarrassing."

"I know."

"Other people can see us."

"I know."

"I want you to kiss me."

"I know." His smile was blatantly sensual. "If I do, I'm not sure I'll be able to stop there. Then we'll both have a problem."

He nearly lost his firm hold on his control when she sighed heavily, her blue eyes clearly showing her disappointment. He brushed his mouth over hers to soothe her and to appease himself. All he accomplished was to fan the flames of sexual attraction flickering between them.

He knew she deserved an explanation for being treated like a blocking dummy, but this wasn't the time or place. Before he did something stupid that might get them arrested, he needed to deal with the reason they had gotten into this position in the first place. His desire for Shay Oakland had almost made him forget he'd just been shot at. It was not only surprising that he could be so easily distracted by Shay, it could be dangerous.

As badly as he would like to stay where he was, he needed to make sure whoever had fired the shot was gone. The only way he could do that was to give the gunman something to shoot at if he was still around. Unfortunately, that was him.

"Stay down by the wall until I tell you it's okay to get up," he ordered as he moved into a crouched position and slowly raised his head to look over the wall.

The stones were cool under his palms as he braced his hands.

His left hand slipped off the wall when Shay touched his shoulder and asked, "Did you lose something?"

Regaining his balance, he glared at her. "Don't do that," he said, his tone rough and low.

Kneeling beside him, she whispered back, "Do what?"

Dillon wasn't sure how to answer that without sounding like a mental defect. He could tell her he was more worried about her welfare than his own. It would be the truth, but he doubted if she would believe him. She was already looking at him as though he were a few cards short of a full deck. He was going to have to give her some sort of explanation. He decided to try the truth, or at least, part of it.

"I heard a gunshot that came from that house next door. I want to make sure whoever shot at me doesn't plan on doing it again anytime soon."

Shay glanced at the house next door, then looked at him with a puzzled expression. "I didn't hear a gunshot."

He stared at her. "You're kidding, right?"

She shook her head. "All I heard was Melba Turnbull's screen door slam shut just before you mistook me for a football and tried to make a touchdown against this wall."

He wanted to believe she was right, but if she was, he was going to come out of this looking like a first-class idiot. "How do you know it was a screen door?"

"The Turnbulls have had the same wooden screen door for as long as I can remember. Melba adds a new coat of dark green paint every September and covers the screen with a storm window every winter. She replaces the springs twice a year because she has six children who wear them out." She turned so she was leaning her back against the wall, and asked, "Why would you automatically assume the sound you heard was a gunshot? Is a jealous husband after you?"

He heard the teasing note in her voice and tried to respond. The sound of his car exploding and broken glass tinkling onto the ground still echoed in his mind. Maybe they always would.

"I don't get involved with married women."

"How commendable," she drawled. "But I think it's more than a cranky husband. A minute ago you said someone was shooting at you, not me or us, but you acted as though you were expecting to be the target. Yesterday you said someone had blown up your car. I was right, wasn't I? You didn't come to Minnesota for the sole reason of talking me into attending the grand opening in Minneapolis or checking up on my late shipment of lingerie."

Dillon stared at her as he debated how much to tell her. He waited too long.

Shay used the wall for support as she stood. Shaking her head, she said, "Never mind. I've decided I don't want to know, after all."

Her lack of interest irritated the hell out of him even though he perversely didn't want to talk about the threats he'd been receiving.

"Why?" he asked as he followed her to the truck.

"Why what?"

"Cadance must be more exciting than I thought if talking about getting shot at doesn't make you even a little curious."

Shay opened the door of the truck and swung up onto the passenger seat. Looking at him, she asked, "Have you ever filled a glass so full it was in danger of spilling over the side if you added one more drop?"

He wondered what a drink had to do with anything. "Once or twice. Why?"

"You are that final drop, Mr. Street. The straw that broke the camel's back, the rain on my parade. I don't have the time or the energy to get involved in your problems. I have a few of my own to deal with."

"Have it your way," he muttered, unreasonably miffed at her cool dismissal of threats against his life. "I wasn't going to tell you about the threats to my life no matter how nicely you asked."

He heard her quick intake of breath and derived some satisfaction from knowing he'd rattled her damned composure.

Chapter Six

Dillon shut the passenger door and walked around the front of the truck. He didn't glance her way when he opened the door on the driver's side, but he was aware she was looking at him. Turning the key in the ignition, he said, "You want me to stop when I see the deputy so you can talk to him?"

"Yes. I last saw Brad about four houses down the street." Pointing to her right, she added, "That way."

Dillon nodded and shifted into reverse.

"Tell me why your car was bombed and your life was threatened." she asked.

"You don't want to know, remember?"

Dillon didn't need to look at her to know she was scowling at him. He could feel her irritation in the air between them. Being aware of what she was feeling was a surprise. Some women were clear as glass to read. Shay Oakland wasn't one of them. She had layers and layers of mystery about her. Yet he was able to read her emotions as though they were his own. The rest—why she and her father were estranged, why she lived in such a remote area—would eventually be explained. He could wait.

The uniformed deputy was coming down the steps of a brick two-story house when Dillon stopped the truck at the curb. Tall and gangly, with a military-style haircut, Brad Knutsen looked like a big kid playing dress-up in his father's clothes. He barely looked old enough to shave. His uniform was spotless and had been pressed meticulously, its creases sharp enough to cut paper. He rested one hand on the butt of the holstered gun worn on his belt. In the other hand he was holding a Mason jar filled with peach and pear preserves as though it would explode at any minute.

Shay had several similar jars on her own pantry shelves courtesy of Mrs. Garner, who lived in the house Brad had just left. Mrs. Garner was generous with her supply of jams and jellies, but stingy with sugar. The woman's preserves could give a lemon competition when it came to tartness.

Shay rolled down the window. "I should have warned you Mrs. Garner still had some preserves left from last fall."

Brad gave the jar a disgusted glance. "I told Mrs. Garner that I was diabetic, but she only patted my arm and assured me fruit was good for me. Last year, her batch of peach and pineapple preserves nearly took the enamel off my teeth. I'm not eating this stuff." The deputy leaned to the side to see the man behind the wheel of her truck. "How do you rate a chauffeur?"

"I don't. This is Dillon Street from San Francisco. Dillon, this is Brad Knutsen, one of my father's deputies."

Both men acknowledged each other with a brief nod, foregoing the ritual handshake, which would have been awkward with Shay between them.

Brad frowned, scowled, removed his cap, and scratched his head while he stared at Dillon. The attempt to physically jog his memory finally paid off. He grinned, his eyes widened, and he slapped his thigh with his cap.

"Shay, that's Dillon Street."

She glanced at Dillon, amusement glittering in her eyes. "Isn't that what I just said?"

"I'd swear to it in court," he replied.

Brad stared at Dillon, but spoke to Shay. "I don't believe it. Dillon Street in Cadance, Minnesota. I just read an article about him in a sports magazine yesterday. No one will ever believe I saw him. Do you think he'd give me his autograph?"

"Why don't you ask him?" suggested Shay. "I understand he speaks English."

The deputy swallowed with difficulty as he leaned down to Shay's window. "Ah, Mr. Street? Would you mind signing an autograph for me? The guys at Har-

ry's Bar and Grill won't believe I really saw you if I
don't have some kind of proof.''

''No problem.'' Dillon leaned forward so he could
reach his wallet in his back pocket. He removed a
business card. Flipping it to the back, Dillon took a
pen from the dash of the truck and wrote on the back.
Then he handed the card to Shay, who in turn passed
it on to Brad.

''Gosh, Mr. Street,'' gushed Brad, who was holding the card as though it was made of delicate glass.
''Thanks.''

Shay marveled at the awe in the younger man's
voice. Hero worship of celebrities had always been a
mystery to her. The well-known entertainers she'd met
through her mother had been people attempting to
have a normal life under extraordinary circumstances. Like her mother, these people made sacri-
fices most people wouldn't consider making to have a
career in a business that dealt out rejection many more
times than it awarded acceptance. They also ex-
changed privacy for living in a public fishbowl surrounded by sharks of all kinds.

''As much as I hate to intrude on this beautiful
moment, Brad, we have a job to do, remember?'' Shay
then told the deputy where she was going. ''With Dillon's help, I'll search the woods while you continue to
check the neighborhood. Quincy suggested we cover
a two-block radius first, then three. If we don't find
Mr. Varanger by late afternoon, we'll call in the volunteer fire department to lend a hand.''

Brad nodded in agreement and, with a shy grin in Dillon's direction, said thanks again and goodbye before heading for the next house.

Dillon murmured, "Sorry about that."

"About what?

"About the autograph."

Shrugging her shoulders, she said, "No problem. It's all part of the game."

"It was at one time," he conceded. "I haven't played football in six years."

"Football isn't the game I meant."

"What did you mean?"

"The public relations game—publicity, advertising, et cetera, ways to keep the star of celebrity shining brightly."

"I'm not going to lie and tell you the publicity my private life gets isn't good for business, but I don't actively go seeking sensationalism. A lot of the stuff printed about me isn't true or even close to the truth. I spend much more time running the stores than I do running after women or attending all-night parties."

Surprised by the defensiveness in his tone, Shay turned her head to look at him. His jaw was clenched, and he was gripping the steering wheel tightly with both hands.

"I didn't mean to be critical of your life. How you live is none of my business. I only meant that I understood about the autograph signing." She glanced briefly at her watch. "We need to get going."

Her attitude was refreshingly different from other women he'd known. In the past, Dillon had put their reactions in two categories. Some were jealous of the attention he got, while others soaked up the notoriety and wanted to be with him because of his reputation, not because of who he was personally. He could be himself with Shay, not a name or an ex-jock or a reputation. His notoriety didn't impress her at all. In fact, she sounded as though she felt sorry for him. Where did that come from? he wondered.

"Dillon?" When he looked at her, she said, "Remember Mr. Varanger?"

"I don't know where Ryerson Woods is."

Shay gave him directions and in a few minutes he was parking the truck at the side of the street bordering a range of trees.

Dillon joined Shay on the sidewalk. Several narrow well-worn paths led the way through thick bushes and stout trees. "You really think the old guy might have wandered into these woods?"

"Call it a hunch or just plain wishful thinking. I would think one of his neighbors would have reported seeing him if he was walking around in the streets. The woods are as good a place as any to look for him."

"I don't imagine I'll run into many elderly men while we're in there, but in case I see more than one, how about telling me what he looks like."

"Mr. Varanger is about my height, very thin, with almost white hair cut very short." She added in a wry tone, "He might or might not be carrying a shotgun."

Dillon paused a step when she reminded him of the gun. "What are the chances he'll use the gun?"

"On us? I don't know. Sometimes he's lucid and sometimes he drifts away into his own world." She raised her hand to hold back a branch in her way as she chose a path into the woods. "Maybe I should let you go first. You're more used to getting shot at than I am."

Dillon chose to ignore her last comment. Her reactions weren't what he'd expected. Hell, he thought, nothing had been as he'd thought it would be since leaving San Francisco. He wasn't sure he was going to tell her the details about the threats he'd been getting. She had enough problems of her own without taking on any of his. Even if he did decide to confide in her, this wasn't the time. What he found strange was her lack of curiosity over his comments about threats and bombs blowing up his car. That type of thing didn't happen to people every day, damn it, he reflected. She could at least show some sort of interest in his safety.

Dillon decided to stick to the path instead of stomping through the underbrush like some heavy-footed Daniel Boone. If the elderly man had difficulty walking, he wouldn't have wandered into the parts of the woods that were thick with weeds and shrubs. The trees were spaced apart so they were able to see around them without too much difficulty. The path was far from a smooth sidewalk, however. A thick carpet of leaves and other debris disguised any dips in the ground, and there were twigs and broken branches, and an occasional stone big enough to twist an ankle if stepped on wrong.

Or cause problems for a knee that had previously been injured, he reminded himself. Dillon stepped carefully over the uneven ground, a part of his mind automatically remembering the necessity of walking carefully. And hating it. He'd basically accepted the injury and his retirement from the game he loved, but he'd never stopped hating the loss of confidence in his athletic ability.

They'd gone about ten feet when Shay said, "I've been thinking."

"I appreciate the warning."

She ignored his comments. "I was right, wasn't I?"

"Probably," he murmured, pushing a tree branch out of his way. "About what?"

"About there being another reason you ventured into the wilderness of Minnesota other than badgering me about attending your grand opening and reminding me my order is late."

Curious as to why she'd chosen this particular time to discuss his problem, Dillon asked, "Why are you bringing that up now?"

"I've been thinking about your strong reaction to the sound you thought was a gunshot. On top of that was the remark about your car being bombed. It's obvious you're in some kind of trouble. Maybe you should talk to Quincy. He might be able to help."

"Your father has enough to cope with for the time being, but I appreciate the offer."

"You have no idea who hates you so much?"

"Believe it or not," he said with a faint smile, "a number of people find me fairly good company. I've even occasionally been invited out to eat without my host worrying if I know how to use a knife and fork correctly."

"I'll take your word for it." Her gaze went to the ground ahead of him. "You might want to watch where you're going. There's a sizable rut several feet ahead of you."

"Thanks," he murmured, stepping over the indention.

Continuing with the subject of the threats and near misses he'd had, Shay said, "Someone thinks they have a good enough motive to go through the trouble to blow up your car. You can't think of a single person who would be happy to see you dead?"

"I had a number of disagreements with various players during games, but we usually hammered out our differences on the field and had a couple of beers together afterward."

"Well, someone has a pip of a grudge against you if he or she is blowing up your car."

He stopped abruptly and turned to look at her. "He or she? Where did the *she* come from?"

"Haven't you ever heard about hell having no fury like a woman scorned? You aren't going to tell me every relationship you've ever had has ended amicably over a couple of beers, too?"

"I hate to burst your feminist little bubble, Shay, but I haven't been seriously involved with anyone since my senior year in college." He began walking along the path again. "That relationship dissolved when she wanted me to use my history degree to become a dignified college professor instead of getting muddy, bloody and bruised in the barbaric game of football." He lifted an arm to shield his face from another branch. "Any other involvement with a woman since has been brief and casual."

"No spurned boyfriend of one of these casual dates? A jealous business competitor, a religious fanatic who thinks lingerie and sporting goods stores are purveyors of sin and corruption?"

"Not that I'm aware of. The written threats weren't signed and if the bomb had a note attached with a signature and an address where we could find the happy bomber, it was blown to bits along with my car."

"What do the police have to say about the chances of finding whoever's responsible?"

"Not much. Flynn has some of his people digging around. So far they haven't come up with anything, but they will keep looking. The police are waiting for something else to happen so they have more to work with."

"Like bullet holes in your anatomy? That doesn't sound fair."

"I didn't think so, either. I decided to take Flynn's advice and disappear while he tries to find the bad guys before they find me. Amy's request to talk to you came at a good time. I could accomplish two things at once."

She didn't understand his cavalier attitude. "You're taking this very calmly."

He shrugged. "I'm not the hand-wringing type. I'm also not stupid enough to stick my head out my door in San Francisco and have it blown off."

He stopped walking suddenly, and Shay almost ran into him.

"What's wrong?"

"I think we've finally found Mr. Varanger," he said in a low voice.

When he stepped forward, Shay was able to see why Dillon had lowered his voice. Arnold Varanger was lying on the ground, his back pressed against a fallen log, his thin body coiled into a fetal position. The shotgun was on the ground beside him. His bare feet were partially covered with leaves.

Dillon knelt down on his good knee and carefully examined the elderly man. In a low voice, Dillon said, "His pulse is steady. Other than being chilled, he doesn't seem to be injured. You get the shotgun. I'll carry him back to the truck."

"Do you think we should move him? I could go after Dr. Pritchard while you stay with him."

"I've had enough experience with how broken bones feel, and he doesn't have any injuries that I can find. It's better to take a chance and move him. He's in more danger of hypothermia. This ground is cold."

She picked up the gun and checked to see if it was loaded while Dillon removed his jacket.

"There aren't any shells in the gun," she said quietly.

Dillon wrapped his jacket around the elderly man and lifted him easily, his weight less than Dillon expected. The movement didn't awaken the elderly man. Dillon could feel Mr. Varanger's body trembling.

"Is there a blanket in your truck?"

"In the back." She stepped around him as she retraced their path into the woods. "I'll run ahead and get it."

Dillon took his gaze off the ground just long enough to get a glimpse of Shay walking away. When he took a step forward to follow her, his foot caught on a large tree root stretched across the path. He came down hard on his right foot and felt the white-hot slash of pain in his knee.

Chapter Seven

Shay held the folded blanket as she waited by the truck for Dillon to emerge from the woods with Mr. Varanger. He seemed to be taking forever, making her wonder if the elderly man had awakened and was giving Dillon a hard time or if Dillon had lost his way. The path was clearly marked to her, but maybe not to him. He was accustomed to street signs and taxicabs, not trees and dirt paths.

She'd made up her mind to see what was keeping him and had taken a step away from the truck when Dillon appeared.

He was carrying Mr. Varanger, who still appeared to be asleep. And Dillon was limping.

Shay's first instinct was to rush to him and offer her assistance, but one glance at his tight jaw and rigid expression stopped her. She'd seen that same closed look often enough from Quincy to recognize it. It was better than a barbed-wire fence for announcing Keep Out.

Without saying a word, Shay stepped around to the back of the truck and opened the tailgate. It took a few minutes to get the elderly man wrapped in the blanket instead of Dillon's jacket and settled on the carpeted flat space behind the seats. Mr. Varanger showed no signs of waking, which began to worry Shay. All the jostling he'd received should have jarred him awake, but it hadn't.

Without being asked, Dillon levered his long length into the back with Mr. Varanger. A muscle in his jaw clenched when he had to bend his bad knee, but he crouched to attend to the unconscious man regardless of the pain. Leaning back against the side window, he cushioned Mr. Varanger's head with his folded jacket and made sure he was covered by the blanket.

Shay hesitated, her blue eyes troubled as she saw Dillon attempt to ease some of the pain in his leg by massaging the muscle above his knee.

He caught her staring and said her name quietly to get her attention. When she looked up, he smiled faintly. "Let's get Mr. Varanger home."

"I'm sorry," she said in a rush. "If you hadn't been helping me, you wouldn't have hurt your leg. It's the knee that you injured in football, isn't it?"

He nodded. "There's one thing you might as well know now, Shay. I rarely do anything I don't want to do. I volunteered to help find Mr. Varanger. You didn't force me to go along."

"You insisted," she murmured.

"Whatever. This old guy could use his own bed about now, and his wife is probably frantic. Let's get going."

Shay nodded and shut the tailgate. Her stomach knotted at the thought of Dillon being in pain, but there was nothing she could do about it. Levering herself up into the driver's seat, she absently rubbed her thigh until she realized what she was doing. *Good Lord,* she thought, *I'm having sympathy pains.*

She used the two-way radio in the truck to call the police station, instructing Jewel to phone Mrs. Varanger, Quincy, Brad, and the Varangers' doctor and tell them that Mr. Varanger had been found. A few minutes' later they arrived at the elderly man's home.

An hour later Shay was behind the wheel again, driving back to Quincy's. Dillon was beside her, unusually quiet since they'd left the Varangers'. Even though she kept her gaze on the road, she was aware of his long fingers massaging his right knee and his thigh as he stared straight ahead. She hadn't inquired if there was anything she could do to make him more comfortable, and he hadn't asked. In fact, he'd said very little from the time he'd carried Mr. Varanger into his bedroom until it was time for them to leave.

Then all he'd asked was "Are you okay to drive home?" which gave her an indication of the pain he was enduring since he didn't assume he would be driving.

She found it difficult to refrain from asking if he wanted to be taken to the emergency clinic. Instead she answered, "I had two cups of Mrs. Varanger's coffee. The caffeine should last long enough to get us to Quincy's without me dozing at the wheel."

She drove back by the same route they'd taken earlier and thought about Dillon's painful knee.

His original knee injury had been serious enough to force him to retire, but that had occurred six years ago. Obviously there were occasions when it still bothered him. Like now.

He hadn't asked for medical treatment when Dr. Pritchard had arrived to check on Mr. Varanger's condition. Dillon hadn't even walked around when the doctor was in the same room. Instead of demanding attention, as some men might, he'd purposely stayed in the background without drawing any attention to himself. While the doctor was checking Mr. Varanger in his bedroom, Dillon sat beside Mrs. Varanger and talked softly to her about the examples of the older woman's needlework in the room. He'd hit on the right topic to draw Mrs. Varanger's attention away from worrying about her husband's condition.

She was going to have to change her preconceived opinion of Dillon Street, Shay realized. He was more complex, more sensitive and caring than she'd expected of the man who had been featured occasionally in tabloids, magazines, newspapers and on television working as a sports commentator during football season. Various articles had emphasized his image as a playboy rather than as a successful businessman, implying he was more interested in playing than working.

Shay should know better than to believe everything she read. Her own mother had received sensational publicity more than once that was grossly unfair and completely untrue. Because she knew the real Monica Sutton, Shay had dismissed the articles as pure rubbish. Perhaps she should give Dillon Street the same benefit of the doubt.

Especially since she had a proposition to make to him.

They were a mile from Quincy's when Dillon finally spoke. "What's going to happen to the Varangers? I heard the doctor tell Mrs. Varanger that she was wearing herself out trying to take care of her husband by herself."

"Their daughter will be coming for a visit in a couple of weeks. Maybe she'll be able to persuade Mrs. Varanger to allow some of her neighbors to help care for her husband."

"Putting him in some sort of medical facility is out of the question, I suppose."

"Mrs. Varanger wouldn't allow anyone to separate them. Dr. Pritchard has suggested it several times, but Mrs. Varanger believes in the marriage vows she took forty years ago."

"Do you?"

"Do I what?"

"Do you believe in love and honor, in sickness and in health, and the rest of it?"

"I haven't thought about it." She shrugged. "Maybe all those things are possible in a perfect world."

"There are few perfect people, but a number of couples manage to have a good life together." His fingers continued to work on the muscles that were tightening up in his thigh. "I think my parents came as close to having a perfect marriage as two people can have. They spent almost all of their time together working in a hardware store they owned in Sunnyvale, California. I'm sure they had disagreements, but they never argued in front of me or my sister. Not once."

Shay thought she knew the answer, but asked the question, anyway. "You describe them in the past tense. Are they still alive?"

He shook his head. "They were in a car accident in Southern California during an earthquake about six years ago. Witnesses said a truck driver either panicked or simply lost control on a freeway when the pavement started shaking. My parents' car was beside the eighteen-wheeler when it tipped over, and they were killed instantly.''

"I'm sorry,'' she murmured. "Is your sister older or younger than you?''

"Two years, three months and fourteen days older.''

Shay chuckled. "You count the days?''

"She does. She always threw those numbers at me like weapons when I didn't do something she told me to do.''

"I'm going to make a wild guess and say that you rarely did as you were told. How close am I?''

Dillon liked the way amusement warmed her blue eyes even when she was laughing at him. "It depended on what she wanted me to do. Would you believe she once tried to make me put on one of her dresses so she could pin the hem up? Sure, you can laugh,'' he complained when Shay did exactly that. "You weren't thirteen with a voice that cracked and a fragile male ego. I'd shot up in height almost overnight to where I was as tall as she was, which was why she wanted to use me as a dressmaker's dummy. When I told her not only no, but hell no, she flung the numbers at me. She was two years, three months and fourteen days older. I was supposed to do what she said because she had been born first.''

"Did you put the dress on?''

He shook his head. "I could run faster than her.''

Shay downshifted as she came to a curve in the road and drove at a slower speed to navigate the bump in the blacktop that was ahead.

Dillon took his gaze off the road and looked at her. "I appreciate the thought, Shay, but if you're taking it easy on my account, it isn't necessary. A few bumps in the road won't make a difference to my knee."

"If you hadn't gone into the woods to help me find Mr. Varanger, you wouldn't have hurt it. I do feel responsible."

"That's not exactly the reaction I was hoping to get from you, but it's better than gushing sympathy or a brush-off for not being perfect."

Shay had the feeling he'd experienced both responses. And hadn't cared for either one. "One thing I learned quickly after Quincy's accident was not to give him any sympathy. As you heard, he accuses me of treating him like a child, when that's exactly how he acts. Maybe I do. I sometimes fall off the fine line he expects me to walk. I'm supposed to help him without making it look like I'm helping. I evidently don't do it very well."

Dillon's smile had a rueful twist. "It's not that easy to be a brave macho male sometimes. We revert back to a primitive caveman occasionally at weak moments."

She smiled as she navigated another curve in the road. "That explains why Quincy threw things the first month he was in the wheelchair."

"I tossed a few items across the room, too, after I was told my career was over because of my knee injury. It was pure frustration. It was a good thing the guy who was the cause of my injury wasn't in the same

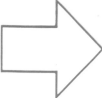

NO COST! NO OBLIGATION TO BUY! NO PURCHASE NECESSARY!

PLAY "LUCKY 7"
AND GET FIVE FREE GIFTS!

HOW TO PLAY:

1. With a coin, carefully scratch off the silver box at the right. Then check the claim chart to see what we have for you—FREE BOOKS and a gift—ALL YOURS! ALL FREE!

2. Send back this card and you'll receive brand-new Silhouette Special Edition® novels. These books have a cover price of $3.50 each, but they are yours to keep absolutely free.

3. There's no catch. You're under no obligation to buy anything. We charge nothing—ZERO—for your first shipment. And you don't have to make any minimum number of purchases—not even one!

4. The fact is thousands of readers enjoy receiving books by mail from the Silhouette Reader Service™ months before they're available in stores. They like the convenience of home delivery and they love our discount prices!

5. We hope that after receiving your free books you'll want to remain a subscriber. But the choice is yours—to continue or cancel, anytime at all! So why not take us up on our invitation, with no risk of any kind. You'll be glad you did!

This lovely heart-shaped box is richly detailed with cut-glass decorations, perfect for holding a precious memento or keepsake—and it's yours absolutely free when you accept our no-risk offer.

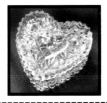

DETACH AND MAIL CARD TODAY

THE SILHOUETTE READER SERVICE™: HERE'S HOW IT WORKS

Accepting free books places you under no obligation to buy anything. You may keep the books and gift and return the shipping statement marked "cancel". If you do not cancel, about a month later we'll send you 6 additional novels, and bill you just $2.89 each plus 25¢ delivery and applicable sales tax, if any.* That's the complete price, and—compared to cover prices of $3.50 each—quite a bargain! You may cancel at any time, but if you choose to continue, every month we'll send you 6 more books, which you may either purchase at the discount price ...or return at our expense and cancel your subscription.

*Terms and prices subject to change without notice. Sales tax applicable in N.Y.

BUSINESS REPLY MAIL
FIRST CLASS MAIL   PERMIT NO. 717   BUFFALO, NY

POSTAGE WILL BE PAID BY ADDRESSEE

SILHOUETTE READER SERVICE
3010 WALDEN AVE
PO BOX 1867
BUFFALO NY 14240-9952

NO POSTAGE
NECESSARY
IF MAILED
IN THE
UNITED STATES

room. I'd be making license plates at San Quentin, serving time for assault."

"I thought breaking a few glasses and cups might help Quincy get rid of some of his anger, so I cleaned up the messes he made without saying anything." She gave him a brief look. "I also made sure he couldn't get to his gun by using the excuse I was taking it to get the firing pin fixed. Now that he seems to have accepted his condition, I felt it was safe to bring his gun back."

Dillon could have argued the point. Quincy had only had two months to adjust. Dillon had had six years, and there were still occasions when his anger was as fresh and raw as it had been shortly after his injury had occurred. He had only just met her father, but Dillon didn't think he was the type to do anything foolish like kill himself.

"Have you been taking care of him by yourself all this time?"

"Some of the objects he threw were aimed at people from town who came out to help. He said they were just curious to find out what kind of shape he was in so they could spread his disability all over town. I was the only one he would tolerate having around."

"And the only one who would take the guff he dished out?"

She smiled faintly. "I suppose so."

Remembering his own initial fury at fate and at the man who had intentionally injured him, Dillon had some idea of the verbal abuse Shay must have endured after Quincy's accident. Dillon knew he himself would have tried the patience of a saint. And his closest friend wasn't even close to being a saintly figure.

"Flynn told me later that he came close to punching my lights out a couple of times when I was behaving like a spoiled brat who'd just been told the party was over. I can't see Quincy being Mr. Congeniality, either."

"Flynn," she repeated. "The private investigator you've known since college?"

"That's the one. I don't know too many people who would have put up with me like he did. He didn't have much time for anyone suffering from self-pity, and he was big enough and tough enough to enforce his opinion that I was acting like a major pain in the butt."

"His method seems to have worked on you. Are you hinting that I should try his techniques with Quincy?"

"No. I'm pointing out that we all can use help once in a while even if we think we don't need it. That includes you just as much as Quincy."

He caught a glimpse of the sun sparkling off the lake through the trees alongside the road and saw the sign advertising a café half a mile up ahead. If he remembered the route correctly, they were fairly close to the turnoff to her father's cabin.

"Stop at the restaurant ahead," he ordered suddenly.

"Why? We're only a few minutes' away from Quincy's. I'll fix something for lunch when we get there."

"I won't be able to say what I want to say at his place. Even I draw the line at propositioning a woman with her father in the room."

Shay made a choking sound that turned into light laughter, which wasn't even close to the reaction he expected. Dillon scowled at her, which made her grin even more.

"Thanks a lot, Shay," he grumbled crossly. "You don't know what it does to a man's ego to have a woman laugh at the idea of being propositioned by him."

"That isn't why I'm laughing." Turning into the parking area in front of a café called Murray's, she pulled into a space and shut off the engine. She unclasped her seat belt and turned partially in the seat to face him. "The reason I was laughing was because we both have the same idea. I planned on propositioning you later."

That shut him up. He didn't have a single word to say on the way into the café.

Shay raised a hand in greeting to several people she knew. But she didn't stop to chat with anyone. Dillon opted for a booth rather than one of the tables, and Shay slid onto the brown vinyl cushion across from him. He had chosen a booth near a window that had red-and-white gingham curtains but didn't have a hanging ivy plant hovering over the table. A plastic red rose had been stuck in a white ceramic bud vase that was surrounded by a variety of bottled condiments. A jukebox at one end of the room was playing a sad country-and-western song.

Dillon propped his right foot onto the seat next to her left hip to ease some of the pressure off his knee. "You go first. I can't remember the last time I was propositioned by a woman."

A woman in a red-and-white gingham uniform with a tiny white apron tied around her generous waist was approaching them with menus in one hand and two glasses of water in the other. A lace handkerchief that was the size of a head scarf stuck out of a breast pocket, fluttering back and forth like a flag with every breath.

Shay shook her head in Dillon's direction and answered, "We'll discuss it after we order."

The waitress plunked the water glasses down and presented the menus with a flourish. Broad in the beam and the chest, the woman was closer to fifty than forty, although in Shay's experiences with the woman, she had the energy and frankness of a ten-year-old. The carrot red color of her hair could only have come from a chemist's bottle, the style of precise curls on top of her head, a couple of decades out of date. Shay knew her to be blunt, brash and bold, but Doris had a kind heart, although she didn't wear it on her sleeve.

"How are ya doin', Shay?" She jerked her head in Dillon's direction. "By the looks of things, you've reeled in a live one."

Shay sighed. "Hello, Doris. This is Dillon Street, who is just passing through, so leave him alone. He's from San Francisco, and he might want to return without being wrung through the wringer and hung out to dry, so be gentle."

"He looks like he can handle himself just fine." Drawing her order pad out of the pocket in the apron, she examined Dillon with a glance as thorough as an X ray. "You look like the kind of man who would fancy a steak as rare as a virgin parked on Lover's Lane," she commented in a voice that nearly rattled the windows. "Murray could slap an inch-thick steak on the grill for you. It comes with a baked potato, string beans, and hot biscuits so light they'll float off your plate. All you have to do is nod your head."

Dillon grinned at the outspoken woman. "As good as that sounds, I'll pass on the steak. I'll take a hamburger with the works and extra pickles and a cup of coffee."

"The works include a thick slice of onion," the waitress warned. "The kind of onions Murray uses could make an angel break into tears. Are you sure you want some on your burger?" She nodded in Shay's direction. "The breath mint hasn't been invented that can counteract the fumes. You might want to think about that if you plan on kissing Shay later."

Dillon's dark eyes narrowed briefly as he stared at Shay, a slow smile shaping his mouth. "You'd better skip the onion, then."

Doris nodded briskly and scratched the pencil across part of the order. "Good choice. What'll you have, Shay?"

"Another waitress," she drawled. "Preferably one that is shy and retiring."

"You know I'm the only one who will put up with Murray's fiery temperament," she said easily, dismissing Shay's complaint. "Speaking of cantankerous old men, how's Quincy?"

"About the same. Would you have Murray do up one of his hamburgers for me to take back for Quincy?" Giving the menu a cursory glance, she added, "I'll have a tuna salad sandwich and a cup of coffee."

The order was scribbled onto the pad. "Got it." She gave Dillon a cryptic smile. "It's going to be about five minutes before I bring your food so you go ahead and get as fresh as you want. Put some color in this girl's cheeks."

"I'll see what I can do," murmured Dillon as he struggled to keep a straight face. "She was about to proposition me, so I might be the one blushing."

The woman's laughter filled every nook and cranny of the dining room, making some of the other customers reach for their vibrating glasses of water. Doris walked away from their booth still chuckling.

Dillon grinned at Shay, who didn't smile back. "That was easy."

"What was easy?"

"Doris wanted some color in your cheeks."

Shay gave him a pained smile. "I thought I was immune to Doris's brand of customer relations."

"She does have a way with words." He paused, his gaze intent on her face. "You said something about a proposition. I'm usually a fairly patient man, but I'm having a hard time waiting to hear what yours is."

She rested her forearms on the table between them and leaned forward slightly. "Between dodging slammed doors that sound like gunshots and having your car bombed, you have implied it is better for your health if you stay out of San Francisco for a while. I need to know if whatever trouble you left behind in San Francisco might follow you here."

"Flynn is the only person other than my secretary who knows where I am. Neither would tell anyone my location even if they were tortured." He briefly told her about the threatening letters, his trashed apartment, and more detail about his car being blown to bits. "Flynn hasn't got much to go on and couldn't be my bodyguard and work on the investigation, too. I didn't notice anyone unusual on the flights I took to get here, so I don't think I was followed. I had a crash course in terrorists' tactics from Flynn so I would understand better how to prevent any of them being used against me. I wasn't followed."

"I know I asked you this before, but I find it hard to believe you have no idea who might want to harm you or why. This guy is very serious. Something had to have set him off."

"I don't know of any disgruntled employees, jealous ex-husbands, dissatisfied customers, or enemies of any kind. Contrary to the tabloids, I lead a fairly dull life. I own the sporting goods stores, which require a great deal of my time. I've decided to give L.L. Bean some competition by starting a mail-order catalog featuring sports equipment. It's what I should be working on right now." His voice hardened. "I hate having my life dictated by some loony."

Shay charged ahead before she changed her mind. "I have a suggestion to make, which would give you a place to stay until you can return to San Francisco. I'd like you to stay with Quincy."

He leaned forward, his forearms resting on the table. "I'm not exactly nursemaid material, Shay. I know what to do for bruises, cuts and pulled muscles from my days playing football, but Quincy's problems are more serious than anything I've ever dealt with before."

"I don't expect you to do anything for him except keep him company. Today was the first time he's shown any animation, any enthusiasm at all, since his accident. I can cook meals for him, give him his medicine, and help him with his therapy, but I can't be a man, and that's what he apparently needs right now."

Dillon shook his head, and Shay's heart sank when she realized he was refusing. She held her hands up in a gesture negating everything she'd just said.

"Never mind. It was a stupid idea."

"It's a brilliant idea," he countered. "And a simple solution. I just wished I'd thought of it."

"You'll stay with him?" she asked cautiously. Part of her wanted him to say no, that he was moving on to another safe haven. That was her sensible nature. Then there was a part of her wanting him to stay even though it could lead to a major complication for both of them. That was her feminine nature.

"Why not?" Shifting his position, he leaned against the back of the booth. "It solves my problem. My proposition was to ask you if I could stay with you, but it would be more sensible to sleep at your father's." He paused for a few seconds, then added, "I couldn't promise to stay out of your bed if I spent the night in your cabin."

And she would be tempted to let him into her bed, she conceded silently. "That was your proposition? You wanted to stay at my house?"

"Oh, I want much more than that, Lady Shay. Wanting you has been automatic since I met you. Lord," he said, exhaling his breath in a drawn-out sigh, "was that only yesterday morning?" He felt his body react when he saw her moist lips part in surprise. "You're another reason I'm not ready to leave here yet, Shay, not just because I was asked to lay low for a while. And it has nothing to do with your work for Dream Street or wanting you at the grand opening. Rockets have never gone off in my bloodstream before when I touched a woman. I think it's worth sticking around to find out what's igniting them and what will happen when they go off." He lowered his voice to an intimate level for her ears only, "I want to be around for the explosion."

Shay felt as though she'd suddenly fallen into a vacuum where there wasn't an ounce of air. Breathing wasn't as easy as it had been a moment ago.

"I'm not going to have an affair with you," she stated abruptly.

"Shay Oakland, have you lost your mind?" boomed Doris as she approached the table with their orders, including a hamburger in a carry-out sack for Quincy. "Having an affair with this good-looking stud is just what you need. Lord, if I was twenty years younger, I'd take a run at him myself."

Dillon's spontaneous laughter irritated the hell out of Shay. It made her wonder how serious he'd been during the last few minutes. She had never felt less like laughing in her whole life.

After Doris placed their plates down in front of them, she said, "You two eat up now. Every bite." Her chuckle sounded like a rasp being dragged across a piece of hardwood. "You're going to need all the energy you can store up for later."

Shay groaned and sank back against the padded cushion of the booth. "Doris, don't you have coffee to pour or tips to count? You're giving Mr. Street the wrong impression."

With one hand on an ample hip, Doris drawled, "Honey, the man already has formed his own impressions and from what I can see, is quite capable of doing something about them. It's you I'm trying to nudge into taking what's being offered. Taking care of Quincy, his place, his job, your own place, and those three mangy mutts is turning you into a hermit. What would your momma say if she saw you right now?"

Shay's frown disappeared, replaced by a smile. "She'd tell me to get my hair and nails done, and lend me one of her sexy expensive dresses before shoving me out the door with orders to have fun or else."

Nodding her head sagely, Doris agreed. "And Monica would be right. Since Quincy's accident you've lost ten pounds and have purple suitcases under your eyes."

"Bags," corrected Shay.

"What?"

"Bags under my eyes. Not suitcases."

"Whatever. You need sleep and some fun. That's all I'm going to say on the subject."

Shay brushed the back of her hand over her forehead as though wiping away perspiration, and said, "Phew, what a relief."

Doris stuck her nose in the air and whirled away from the booth, mumbling, "That's the thanks I get for trying to help."

Dillon's gaze followed the waitress for a few seconds. Then he brought his attention back to Shay. Grinning, he said, "I'd better leave her a big tip to cheer her up."

"If she was any happier, she'd be turning cartwheels. Waiting on tables is only a sideline for Doris.

Butting her nose into other people's business has been her main occupation for as long as I've known her."

"She's very good at it. She's also right about you needing some sleep."

Shay picked up a piece of tuna that had fallen out of the sandwich onto the plate, popping it into her mouth. "Don't let her hear you say that. She always thinks she's right."

Dillon's expression had sobered, his eyes concerned. "I'm serious."

"So am I. You don't know her like I do."

"I meant about your being worn out."

"Don't sugarcoat your compliments, Maverick," she said dryly. "Come right out with them. It's a surefire way to turn a girl's head to tell her she looks like hell."

"That's not what I said," he murmured through clenched teeth. "You couldn't look like hell if you hadn't slept for a month." After a long pause, he asked, "Why is it so difficult for you to accept that someone could care enough to be worried about you?"

She blinked, startled by his question. "You don't know me well enough to know how I feel about anything. Are you going to eat that hamburger or continue scowling at me while I eat this sandwich?"

"I might do both. Lord, you're one stubborn lady." He picked up the hamburger in two hands. "To show you how cooperative I can be, I'll change the subject.

Why isn't your mother here helping you take care of your father?"

Shay nearly choked on the bite she'd taken out of the sandwich. She coughed several times and took a long sip of water before she was able to answer him.

Dillon left his seat to pat her heartily on the back. Instead of returning to the other side of the booth, he slid onto the bench she was sitting on. He rubbed the palm of his hand gently over her back. "Better?"

"Have you ever heard of making polite conversation?"

"For one thing, talking about the weather or other inane subjects is boring. For another, I want to know more about you, and since you haven't volunteered much about yourself, I have to ask questions."

"I think we should get a few things straight," she said uneasily. He was too close, much too close. "Asking you to stay with my father will benefit both him and you. And to be honest, me, too. He'd have some male company and you would have a place to stay until it's safe for you to go back to San Francisco. Sleeping with me is not part of the deal."

"I'll break this to you as gently as I can, Shay," he said in a soft drawl. "You *are* the deal. Cadance, Minnesota, isn't the only place I could go until it's safe to return home. But you are here. So this is where I'm staying."

Shay suddenly felt claustrophobic, as though the walls were closing in. He was crowding her, physically, mentally, and emotionally, pressing too hard, too fast. His nearness was threatening. So was her reaction. Her common sense told her it was impossible to be so strongly attracted to a man she'd known for such a short time. But her body didn't care about intelligent arguments. She ached to have him touch her, to feel his firm mouth claiming hers. She tried to convince herself that it would be disastrous to let herself become intimately involved with him.

Her traitorous body wasn't convinced.

Leaning against the back of the booth, she shook her head. "I thought your reputation had been exaggerated by the press. Evidently the reporters knew what they were talking about when they described your reputation with women. You expect me to fall into bed with you just because for the moment you've decided you want me."

"I have a feeling I'm going to want you longer than for a moment," he murmured as he reached for the back of her neck.

"This is crazy," she breathed haltingly. "We hardly know each other."

"Physically, we seem to be on the same wavelength whether you want to believe it or not. I wanted you three seconds after the first time I saw you," he said in a matter-of-fact tone. Then he smiled, his fingers playing with the strands of silky hair flowing over his hand. "If you think that's crazy, you're going to have a fit when I tell you I know you're attracted to me, too."

Shay stared at him, wishing with all her heart she could tell him he was wrong. She knew, and unfortunately so did he, that she'd be lying.

Rubbing her forehead in an attempt to erase the headache throbbing again in her temples, she murmured, "Maybe I'm just having a bad dream. This really isn't happening at all. I'll wake up and everything will be back to normal."

"Poor baby," he said soothingly. Touching her chin with his fingers, Dillon turned her to face him. "Let me kiss you and make it better."

His mouth covered hers with a possessiveness that stunned him almost as much as it did her. There was nothing tentative or teasing about his claim. He took her taste into his mouth and savored her sensual response.

He applied pressure with his hand on her back, bringing her breasts into his chest. Dillon groaned softly and deepened his claim on her mouth.

Shay leaned into him, unable to fight both him and her rampaging need. She held on to his shoulders as he dragged her down into a whirlpool of sensation. She was lost in the heated depths of a desperate need unlike anything she'd ever experienced. There had never been anything she'd craved like this, never anyone who brought her body alive with an aching pleasure. The other patrons, Doris, everyone and everything, ceased to exist. She was aware only of Dillon and the explosion in her bloodstream.

She made a sound of protest when he broke away from the intimate assault on her mouth. With a hand on the back of her head, Dillon pressed her face into the curve of his neck and shoulder. She could feel his pulse racing and touched her moist lips to the pounding vein in his neck. He shuddered against her, and he tightened the hold he had on her. She was aware that his breathing was as ragged and rough as hers.

In a voice husky with desire, Dillon murmured, "We'd better get out of here before Doris has to pour a bucket of cold water over us to cool us off."

Dillon removed a money clip from his pocket, peeled off a twenty-dollar bill, and dropped it on the table. Then he slid out of the booth and leaned down to take her hand. Tugging on it gently, he said, "Come on, sweetheart. Let's get you to bed."

Dillon was nearly toppled over onto the table when a heavy hand slapped him in the middle of the back.

"Now you're talking, young man," bellowed Doris as she passed the booth.

Chapter Eight

The short drive to Quincy's cabin was made in silence. Shay had no idea what Dillon was thinking, but she was fully aware of the direction her own thoughts were going in. She was desperately trying to catch up to Dillon, who had raced ahead to put their relationship on a more intimate level.

She was also aware she hadn't told Dillon to take his proposition and jump into the lake with it. She was seriously considering having an affair with a man she'd known for two days! she realized. It was unfortunate she hadn't bumped her head when he'd tackled her on Mrs. Varanger's lawn. Then she could blame her actions on brain damage. Since that wasn't the case, she had to accept the startling fact that she wanted him.

She actually wanted a man she'd met less than seventy-two hours ago.

Maybe she was like her mother, after all, she thought. Except Monica married the men she was attracted to instead of having an affair with them. Shay was certain marriage was the last thing on Dillon Street's mind. Which brought her right back to the two choices she had: to have an affair or not.

She was no closer to an answer when they arrived at Quincy's cabin.

When they entered the living room, Quincy turned off the television show he'd been watching and waited for a report on Mr. Varanger. Shay gave the sack containing a hamburger to her father and told him that Dr. Pritchard said the elderly man was going to be all right, at least physically. That out of the way, she approached her father with the idea of Dillon spending the night at his cabin. She carefully worded the suggestion to encompass only one night in case the arrangement didn't work out.

Quincy immediately approved without any hesitation and extended an open invitation for the ex-football player to stay as long as he wanted.

Shay tried not to be hurt when Quincy proceeded to ignore her and spoke only to Dillon from then on. She evidently hadn't been forgiven for her part in their argument. If Quincy was waiting for her to apologize, he was in for a long wait. To keep the peace, she usually did. But this time she had meant every word. Perhaps she could have been more tactful in telling him he needed to start learning to take care of himself instead of relying on her for everything. But she'd been tired and irritable, which made what she'd said come out harsh instead of helpful.

Shay could have reminded Quincy that he had flung a number of painful darts in her direction, too. He hadn't liked it when she had argued that his complaint that she stop treating him like a child was similar to what she was trying to point out to him. He wanted more independence, and she wanted him to start doing more for himself. It had been stupid to argue when they both wanted the same thing.

Unfortunately the initial argument had led to dredging up the past, using it as a weapon in a battle neither could win.

The arrangements for Dillon to stay had nothing to do with her bruised feelings, she told herself. By asking him to stay, she was insuring that Quincy would have someone with him whose company he enjoyed. Maybe Dillon wouldn't appreciate the position of caretaker she'd put him in, but she had also done him a favor by arranging for a place for him to stay until it was safe for him to return to San Francisco.

Shay chanced a glance in Dillon's direction and found he was watching her, his usual amused expression replaced by a puzzled frown. She couldn't blame him if he was having second thoughts about his decision to stay with Quincy.

She was oddly hesitant about leaving them alone together. The only reason she could think of for her reluctance was her feeling that she was abandoning a helpless bird in a nest before he'd learned to fly. Although thinking of Dillon Street as a helpless anything was quite a stretch. The real reason was, she had liked feeling needed. Quincy had depended on her for so long, caring for him had become part of her daily life. He'd accused her of treating him like a child, so it was important for her to back away and give him room. She just hadn't expected to feel so useless.

Dillon came over to her. Putting his hand on her arm, he drew her along with him to the door facing the lake. "Will you be all right going home in the boat?"

She blinked. "Of course." She turned a similar question back on him. "Are you going to be all right here with Quincy?"

He smiled. "Of course." He gave her a gentle push toward the door. "Go get some sleep. Your father and I are adults, Shay. Stop worrying and go home."

Quincy didn't even look at her when Shay mentioned she'd return later to fix their dinner, nor did he watch her as she left the cabin.

Dillon did. In fact, he followed her progress across the lake from the window until he saw her tie up her boat at her dock. Using the binoculars he found on the windowsill, he saw her stand at the end of the dock staring in his direction. He knew she couldn't possibly see him from so far away. Yet he felt as though she was looking into his eyes, into his soul, into the private inner passages he allowed very few people to see or touch. Shay Oakland had found her way there effortlessly the moment she'd first met his eyes and smiled. That realization should have scared the hell out of him, but for some strange reason, it didn't.

The memory of the kiss they'd shared was suddenly so intense, he sucked in his breath as he was rocked by a tidal wave of desire. When Shay turned and walked toward her cabin, he was finally able to break away.

Putting the binoculars back where he'd found them, Dillon turned to his host. He would like to ask Quincy what was causing the animosity between him and his daughter, but Dillon decided to wait until he knew Quincy longer than fifteen minutes before he interfered. He'd give it maybe half an hour.

He looked over at Shay's father, who had positioned his wheelchair near the couch. "She made it to her place without any problems."

"I would be amazed if she hadn't. She's been around boats since she was six years old."

"Is that when you bought the lake?"

Quincy shook his head. "Saber Lake has belonged to my family for three generations . Shay lived with her mother in California before I brought her here when she was six."

If Dillon was reading the older man's expression correctly, Dillon was treading into territory that was out of bounds. He would leave the subject of Shay's past alone for now.

"Are you a betting man, Quincy?"

The older man's eyes widened, clearly surprised by the change of subject. "I have been known to be if the stakes are right. Why?"

"Do you have a deck of cards?"

Quincy nodded and hitched a thumb in the direction of the desk. "In the second drawer on the left."

Crossing the room, Dillon opened the drawer Quincy had indicated. He found the deck of cards and slid them out of the box.

"When the team went to training camp or to away games, we were assigned roommates," he stated as he casually strolled back to the sofa. "The guys played poker as a way to divide up the work, especially the chores no one wanted to do."

"Why are you telling me this?"

Dillon heard the impatience in the older man's voice. He detected a hint of curiosity, as well. "We don't want your cabin to start looking and smelling like a locker room after a game. It's not fair to expect Shay to pick up after us when we're capable of doing the chores ourselves. I plan on doing my share, but not everything."

"Now look—" snapped Quincy, but Dillon ignored his outburst.

"Each hand of poker we play will be for a particular job like making beds or cooking breakfast. Whoever loses has to do that chore."

Quincy's face took on an ominous expression. "If you're attempting to be funny, you aren't succeeding, young man. I'm in a wheelchair. I can't do anything."

Dillon spoke one word, a pungent two-syllable word straight out of a barnyard. Perhaps if anyone else had said such a word to Quincy, he would have reacted with the hard edge of his temper. Maybe it was Dillon's challenging smile accompanying the word that tempered Quincy's reaction.

Still angry, Quincy asked, "All right, smart guy, since you think you have all the answers, exactly how am I supposed to do my share of the work around here when I'm in this chair?"

"If you don't know how to do stuff around the house or you can't cook, say so. Some men have problems doing what they consider women's work. If that's—"

"I raised a child since she was six years old, along with holding down a full-time job, so don't patronize me, Maverick," Quincy said indignantly. "I was the only cop on the force who had permanent dishpan hands, but that was before I ended up in this chair."

"Your brain still works. So do your arms and hands. You'll figure something out."

"You don't know what the hell you're asking me to do."

"Don't I? I bet I can come damn close." The light tone he'd been using changed to a hard, flinty monotone. "One minute I was full of adrenaline after catching a perfectly thrown pass and running through a field of uniformed bodies toward the goalpost. The next thing I knew I was on a stretcher. I remember waking up in a hospital feeling as though my knee had been seared by a white-hot bolt of lightning. It took a while for me to realize I'd been seriously injured. It was even longer for me to accept my career was over.'' He snapped his fingers. ''Just like that, my whole life was changed dramatically and irrevocably, and I'd had no control over any of it happening. The only choice I had was to accept it and find a way to work around it.''

The older man's gaze never left Dillon's face the entire time. ''At least you can walk. You had options I'll never have.''

''But I can't run,'' stated Dillon flatly. ''I'll never pit myself against another team, another opponent. Football was my life. The hardest thing I've ever had to do was accept that I would never play again. Once I finally managed to do that, I was able to go on. I concentrated on what I could do instead of dwelling on what I couldn't do. You might want to give it a try.''

Quincy's face registered a variety of emotions as he thought over what Dillon had admitted. Dillon didn't add anything else to what he'd already said. He let the silence continue as long as Quincy needed it.

Four minutes dragged by before Quincy propelled the chair toward the low table in front of the couch. His voice firm, he murmured, ''I used to be a pretty fair poker player. You might want to change the stakes.''

Dillon grinned as he fanned the deck of cards from one hand to the other with the flare of a riverboat gambler. "I'll take my chances."

"I think I'm in trouble," Quincy muttered.

Dillon sat down on one of the cushions of the couch and spread the cards out in a curved row, facedown. "High card deals."

Quincy picked a card and flipped it over. It was a jack of diamonds. His smile was smug, a hint of a challenge in his eyes.

Dillon chose a card and turned it over. It was the king of spades. Quincy's smile faded but the challenge remained.

Gathering up the cards, Dillon shuffled them quickly and expertly before he started to deal. "Five card stud, nothing wild. Loser has to take out the garbage."

Quincy picked up the five cards Dillon had dealt to him. "You're on." After arranging the cards to suit him, he said casually, "Somewhere down the line, we'll have to play for information, like what you're really doing in the backwoods of Minnesota so far away from your usual action."

Dillon paused briefly, then removed two cards from his hand. "I wouldn't say there's no action here. When I arrived at your daughter's cabin, her three dogs wanted to make me into prime doggie chow. Then she strapped on your gun before taking me on a fun-filled water ride. After that, we stomped through some trees to find an elderly man curled up like a baby with a shotgun beside him. We stopped at Murray's Café where a redheaded steamroller called Doris ran over me a couple of times and nearly broke my eardrums. Yeah, it's been pretty boring so far."

"So what Shay said about you being here to persuade her to go to some grand opening is the only reason you're here?" He shook his head. "She might buy that, but I don't."

"Now I know where she gets her suspicious nature. She didn't accept it, either," Dillon complained. "How many cards do you want?"

"I'll play these. So what's the real reason you're sticking around other than the fact you're attracted to my daughter?"

Dealing himself two cards, Dillon didn't bother denying Quincy's remark about his attraction to Shay. Discussing the desire to sleep with a woman with her father, however, was a bizarre enough situation to be uncomfortable. He decided to tell Quincy about the threats he'd received instead. Shay's father was an experienced lawman and might have some insight into his problem that hadn't occurred to Flynn or to him. Plus, Dillon wanted Quincy to know the truth behind his trip to Minnesota. He honestly didn't think his enemy could track him to Quincy's cabin, but Dillon felt it was only fair the older man knew the potential danger.

But before he could say a single word, his host spread his hand out on the table and announced, "Full house."

Dillon tossed his hand onto the table. All he had was a pair of threes. He was now in charge of taking out the garbage.

While Quincy shuffled the deck, Dillon began to relate the sequence of events surrounding the threats to his life, starting with the first letter he'd received. When Dillon reached the part about his car being blown up, thankfully without him in it, he noticed Quincy had stopped fiddling with the cards and was listening intently.

Shay felt as though her eyelids were made of sandpaper when she finally managed to open her eyes. When she was able to focus with some degree of accuracy, she glanced at the small bedside clock. She blinked and looked again. It couldn't be ten o'clock, she thought. That would mean Quincy and his houseguest had gone without dinner, unless Dillon knew his way around a kitchen.

Staring at the ceiling, Shay noticed there seemed to be a lot of light in the room considering the time of night. Turning her head on the pillow, Shay looked at the window and saw sunlight filtering through the drapes.

There was only one explanation that made any sense. It wasn't ten o'clock in the evening. It was ten o'clock in the morning. She'd slept all afternoon and through the night.

She groaned, rolled over, and buried her face in her pillow. It was the first time she hadn't fixed her father's evening meal since his accident, except the night after their argument. She'd always stayed until he fell asleep, using that time to tidy his cabin.

When she eventually returned to her own home, she would sew until her eyes and her fingers burned. Whatever spare time she had found to work on her designs for Dream Street hadn't been enough to complete them. The deadline had passed for the designs to be sent in, and she hadn't finished them yet. There just never seemed enough time in the day or night to get everything done. Now it looked as if she was going to have to make the time. With Dillon staying with her father even for a couple of nights, she would be able to work more hours, possibly even catch up on her orders.

Rolling onto her back, Shay stared up at the ceiling. Dillon Street. Yesterday it had seemed like a brilliant solution to have Dillon stay at Quincy's, someone whom her father would tolerate. The ex-football player had made quite an impression on Quincy just by walking into his cabin.

Her mouth twisted. She imagined Dillon made that kind of impact wherever he went. She hadn't been immune to his charm, either, she admitted. And it had absolutely nothing to do with football. Reaching for her other pillow, she wrapped her arms around it and hugged it against her aching breasts. Damn him, she cursed silently. She didn't want to be attracted to a celebrity, to a man who took very little seriously, especially himself.

Although he did seem to be taking the threats on his life with more than a casual interest, she reminded herself. Nothing like a bomb exploding in a car to get someone's attention. The occasional anonymous threat was usually accepted as part of the game when someone was a celebrity. Her mother had received her share from jealous women and desperately lonely men over the years. Someone hadn't stopped at threats with Dillon, however. A bomb planted in his car couldn't be dismissed easily.

Yesterday she hadn't asked for many details of the trouble he was in. One question she had asked, he hadn't answered—about if there was a remote chance his enemy could track him to Cadance. Dillon had told her that his friend Flynn and his secretary were the only people who supposedly knew where he'd gone. She could only hope he was right. She didn't want to have provided her father with company who could put him in danger, especially now when Quincy was vulnerable and unable to defend himself.

Shay tossed the pillow aside, then the covers. As tempting as it was to pull the blankets over her head, she was going to face the day and all the problems that came with it. According to the clock, she was twelve hours overdue at her father's as it was.

A half hour later, Shay tugged the banded hem of a white cotton sweater over tan chambray-clad hips. She shoved the sleeves up to just below her elbows and debated about French-braiding her hair or simply securing it at the base of her neck. A quick glance at the

clock made up her mind for her. The intricate braid-
ing took too much time and patience, neither of which
she had to spare that morning. She settled for a mock
tortoiseshell barrette to hold her hair securely at the
nape of her neck.

At least she felt more in control and not so dopey
from weariness after catching up on some sleep. She
even felt ready to face the challenge of seeing Dillon
Street again.

Shay smiled faintly at her reflection in the full-
length mirror on the closet door as she thought of her
mother's reaction if Monica could see Shay wearing
what the actress termed "tacky country attire." Even
though Shay hadn't lived with her mother for twenty-
three years, she had spent enough time with Monica
Sutton to know the woman's opinions on presenting
the proper appearance at all times. Especially in front
of men. Shay smiled. This outfit wasn't even close.

Monica would have a fit Bette Davis-style if she
could see Shay now. The casual pants, oversize sweater
and white running shoes were comfortable and certainly weren't the type of clothes to choose if she was
trying to attract a man.

She hadn't felt this ridiculous since she was an
awkward teenager with a crush on Taylor Alexander,
who didn't even know she existed. That was when she
was thirteen, pretending she wasn't interested in a guy
when she was. Now at age twenty-nine, she was doing
the same thing.

She turned away from the mirror. She was losing her mind. That explained everything. Yesterday she could blame her reaction to him on a lack of sleep. She didn't have that excuse today. Nor could she use the fact they'd known each other only a short time. The attraction had sprung up between them as suddenly as a spring rain. She had to decide what she was going to do when desire became an uncontrollable storm.

The sun was glittering like thousands of tiny stars dancing on the dark blue water as she directed the boat toward Quincy's dock. As usual, the lake and the surrounding area were peaceful and quiet. Close to the dock, she cut the engine and drifted. No one came out on the deck when she tied up the boat at the dock. Once the boat was secured, she walked up the grass-covered shoreline. The glass in the windows was intact and everything seemed to be normal. The two men had evidently survived the night without Quincy throwing furniture or Dillon through the window.

She let herself in and glanced around the empty living room. The only thing she could see out of place was a deck of cards on the coffee table. The clatter of metal scraping against metal drew her toward the kitchen.

She stopped abruptly in the doorway to take in the scene in front of her. Quincy was seated in his wheelchair near the table, his elbow on the armrest as he repeatedly lifted and lowered a strange-looking weight in his hand. Even more startling was the fact he was dressed in jeans and a plaid flannel shirt. It was the first time she'd seen him in anything other than pajamas and robe since his accident.

Dillon's back was to her as he stood at the sink, his arms elbow-deep in sudsy water. As she stepped farther into the room, she saw Dillon had tucked a dish towel into the waistband of a pair of jeans. Also, he was wearing a different shirt than the one he'd worn yesterday, this one an off-white sport shirt with vertical tan stripes. He must have used Quincy's truck to get his suitcase from the car stuck in her lane, she thought.

"Good morning," she murmured to the room in general.

Dillon glanced at her over his shoulder. "Good morning. Do you want some coffee? Quincy just made a fresh pot, and I guarantee one sip of the mud he calls coffee would wake up the dead."

Quincy had made the coffee, was dressed in regular clothes, and was exercising without being browbeaten, bribed, or threatened. In less than twenty-four hours, Dillon had worked miracles. She wasn't proud of the resentment she was feeling toward him for accomplishing in one day what she hadn't been able to do in two months. The important thing was that Quincy was finally coming to life again.

She looked at her father. His face was flushed from the exertion of lifting the strange weights. "I've had Quincy's coffee before. I'll pass." She stepped closer to examine the peculiar-shaped weight he was lifting.

"Where did you get this? It looks like a sock filled with sand."

Quincy stopped pumping his right arm and switched the floppy weight to his left. "That's because it's a sock filled with sand. Wet sand. Dillon rigged it up and weighed it on the bathroom scale. Five pounds exactly. The other weights I had were too heavy to start out with."

She looked over at Dillon, who was drying his hands on the towel at his waist. "You've been busy. Would you mind sharing your secret of how you persuaded Quincy to get dressed, make coffee, and exercise?"

"Poker."

She blinked. "Excuse me?"

"We played poker. You know, the card game. Full house, three of a kind. He lost the hand where we bet he'd get rid of the jammies during the day, and won the round for making coffee." Tugging the dish towel from his waist, he added, "As you can see, I lost the bet about washing the breakfast dishes."

Shay stared at him, then shifted her gaze to Quincy, who was grinning back at her with that quirky twist to his mouth she hadn't seen since the accident. During the past two months, she'd tried coaxing, nagging, begging, even bribery, without much success. Gambling had never occurred to her.

"It looks like I was fretting for nothing when I woke up this morning and realized I hadn't made dinner last night. You two seem to have managed just fine."

"So far," agreed Dillon as he narrowed his gaze and studied her expression. She looked like someone who had just had her toes stepped on. "We managed to stave off starvation."

"He's being modest, Shay," her father said. "He threw together a casserole last night he called tuna surprise."

"Quincy, you hate tuna. There isn't any tuna in the cupboards to make a casserole."

Her father's smile widened. "That's the surprise. There wasn't any tuna in it. I never thought noodles and mushroom soup would be good, but I ate two helpings."

"I'll have to get his recipe," she said dryly. "Have either of you checked with Travis this morning to find out when he can come after Dillon's car?"

"That's taken care of, Shay," said Dillon. "He brought the car around last night. Aside from being covered in dust, there isn't any damage to the engine or the frame, so the rental company won't have to sue me."

"Then you can leave at any time."

He gave her a crooked smile. "Quincy has invited me to stay as long as I want, remember?" He held up his hand, palm out, to ward off any complaint she might make. "Think about it. I can help Quincy with his therapy and keep myself in one piece while Flynn is investigating the car bomb and the threats."

Shay glanced at Quincy. "Dillon told you about his problem?"

Her father nodded. "That's when I repeated my offer to put him up however long it takes to catch the guy. I can't think of any place safer. No one would suspect the Maverick would travel to this area voluntarily. Even if his enemy did discover he was here, he would have me, my police force, and my revolver to protect him."

"This arrangement would also help you out, Shay," Dillon added. "You will have more time to work on your order for Dream Street."

She could feel Quincy's gaze on her, but she didn't look his way. Both men had valid arguments in favor of Dillon's plan to stay with Quincy. It was obvious the retired football player was good for her father. Dillon had accomplished more in the past twenty-four hours than she had in that many days.

She nodded. "If you're going to be staying for a while, you should learn how to run a boat. I don't have a telephone. And I might not hear the two-way radio if you try to reach me in an emergency. I would feel better if you had a way of contacting me by crossing the lake. Driving around the lake to reach my lane takes about thirty minutes." She smiled faintly. "Then you'd have to drive up the lane, which you might not want to try again."

Dillon frowned. She was right. It would be more practical to be able to go across the lake instead of the long way around by car to reach her cabin.

"Quincy's boat is in the boathouse and is almost exactly like the one I use," she continued. "Once you learn how to operate mine, you could take his out."

"All right," he said grudgingly. "When do you want to show me the ropes? No pun intended."

"How about right now?"

He looked at her steadily, aware of the tension stiffening her spine. He got the impression she wanted to get him away from the cabin and Quincy's presence. He also had a fair idea what she wanted to talk about.

While the boat was still tied up to the dock, Shay ran through the basic operating instructions, pointing out gauges, the compass, the throttle. She didn't go into detail about how things worked, only what the various instruments were used for and why he should know how to use them.

When she indicated the compass, he asked, "Why would I need a compass? Your place is the only other one on the lake." He pointed. "And it's over there."

Shay moved his arm about five inches to his left. "My cabin is there. What would you do if there was a thick bank of fog covering the lake and you couldn't see my cabin?"

"I wouldn't go out on the lake."

"What if there was an emergency and I didn't respond to the radio?"

He grinned. "I'd follow the compass heading you're going to give me."

"You catch on quickly."

"I'm not so sure," he grumbled. "I've been with you for over an hour and I haven't kissed you yet. I'm slowing up."

"Oh, I don't think so," she murmured. "If you moved any faster, I'd get whiplash."

Any sign of humor had disappeared. "I've been giving you time to adjust to the idea of sleeping with me. Your time is about up."

"Why don't you let your motor idle for a while and concentrate on the one in the boat? I'll cast off the lines while you start the engine. You might want to wait until I join you in the boat before you put it in gear."

She started to walk to the stern of the boat when he caught her wrist. "You can't keep running away from me, Shay. I won't let you. Even with a bum knee, I'll catch you."

"What if I don't want to be caught?"

His thumb was stroking across the vein in her wrist as he searched her eyes. He was pleased to feel her pulse quicken.

"Tell me you don't want me to touch you. Tell me you haven't wondered what it would be like to feel me inside you." Her pulse jumped violently. "Tell me you don't want me, Shay."

"I can't," she breathed.

He smiled slowly and released her wrist. "Have you ever made love in your boat?"

Shay shook her head slowly, amazed she could accomplish even that simple motion. He looked so damn smug, she thought. She had an irrational desire to shake him up a little.

Moving away to the stern, she looked at him over her shoulder. "Not yet," she said softly.

Dillon groaned. It wouldn't take much for him to pull her down on the deck and end the aching desire knotting his gut. The thought of Quincy picking up his binoculars off the windowsill was stopping him.

The throaty purr of the inboard motor leveled out when Dillon followed the instructions Shay had given him. Once away from the dock, he made several sedate trips back and forth across the lake. The wind tugged at his hair and his shirt when he tapped the throttle to increase the speed. He half closed his eyes as the fine spray hit his face as the boat cut across the smooth surface of the lake.

Since he appeared to be enjoying handling the boat, Shay was surprised when he lowered the speed in the middle of the lake. When the boat was barely crawling along, Dillon shut off the engine, letting the boat drift.

"You aren't going to try that old line about running out of gas, are you?" she asked, amusement tugging at the corners of her mouth.

He shook his head. "That wouldn't work with you. Besides, I'd choose somewhere a lot more private than the middle of a lake. Your father has some high-powered binoculars and a gun. This isn't the time or the place to find out how quickly I could make you respond to me when I touch you."

Shay smiled. "You're like a kid with a sweet tooth who has had just about every kind of candy there is, yet you want more."

"You think you know me so well, don't you?" he snapped, not a trace of amusement in his voice or his eyes. "You read a couple of articles about me and came to the conclusion I'm a bed-hopping jackrabbit. I thought you were smarter than that." He put his hand on the ignition key. "I thought you were fairer than that. I guess I was wrong."

Before he could restart the engine, Shay put her hand on his arm. "I'm sorry, Dillon. You're right. I wasn't being fair." After a brief pause, she admitted, "You scare the hell out of me."

He was stunned by her admission. "Why?"

She stared out over the water. "I spent a couple of weeks with my mother at a resort in Florida when I was thirteen or fourteen. While we were there, a hurricane was brewing off the coast and my mother was advised to leave, to go inland where we would be safe. You would have to know Monica to realize being safe has never been one of her priorities." Shay turned to meet Dillon's piercing gaze. "You remind me of that hurricane. You blow into the area, stir things up, then you go somewhere else. It's your nature. You won't intentionally hurt anyone, but you won't be aware of any devastation you've left behind because you'll be gone. I'm not like my mother, Dillon. She stood at the end of a pier and faced the direction the hurricane was coming from, daring it to do its worst. She tried to make me face the storm, too, but I shut my eyes."

"She made you go out on the pier with her even though she knew you were frightened?"

"Monica honestly thought she was teaching me to face adversity and not run away from things just because they had become difficult."

"Your mother should have met my grandfather. He threw me into a lake when I was four to teach me how to swim. I sank like a rock and nearly drowned."

Shay smiled faintly. "I was sick all over Monica's French silk shoes."

"Good for you." Dillon's gaze remained fixed on Shay for several minutes before he spoke again. "I'm not a threat to you, Shay. I'm attracted to you. Hell, I lie awake at night aching to make love to you. I wish I could tell you how long it will last, but I don't know. I've never felt as though the world as I know it will end if I never make love with you."

"I believe you wouldn't intentionally hurt me or Quincy, but it's inevitable. You've changed Quincy from a depressed invalid into a man with life dancing in his eyes again. If you and I become lovers, how am I supposed to live with the fact I went against my own rules and had a one-night stand?"

"I can't make any promises for more than an affair," he warned.

"I don't expect any empty promises. But I need to keep the ones I made to myself."

"What about the way we make each other feel? Can you just pretend it doesn't exist?"

"No," she breathed. "I wish I could."

"Whoever is behind the threats and blowing up my car has no idea of the favor he did me. I might not have realized how valuable every day was until I discovered someone was trying to make sure I didn't have too many of them left."

"Live for today and to hell with tomorrow? I don't think that would work for me."

"My mother once said I hit the ground running from the day I was born. She's probably right. I've always been impatient when there's something I've wanted. That's even more true since I've been receiving those threats."

"Does it matter to you if others might not want the same thing?"

"Are we talking about Quincy or us?"

"There is no us yet, so I must be talking about my father. You've done so much for him in such a short time. Quincy hated the way he was. I knew that, but I didn't know how to go about changing things. You did. You knew how to let him keep his pride and change his attitude. He was right. I have treated him like a child and held him back."

"Don't be so hard on yourself. I've had more experience in dealing with frail male egos, including my own, than you have, that's all."

"I haven't thanked you for what you've done for Quincy."

"You'd better not thank me yet."

"Why not?"

"I have purely selfish motives for wanting to help your father learn how to take care of himself."

"Like what?"

"If he's more independent, he'll be less dependent on you. You've been running yourself into the ground trying to do everything for him without allowing any time for yourself."

"And what would I do with this free time? Perhaps go to Minneapolis with you for the grand opening?"

He shook his head. "I've been talking to Quincy. He doesn't think I should appear at such a public event until the person making the threats has been caught and stopped. He gave me a different idea for publicity instead of personal appearances by the designers."

Cautiously, Shay asked, "I'm going to hate myself for asking, but what was Quincy's suggestion?"

"To have a photographer go to the designers and take pictures of them at work. I thought we would start with you."

Chapter Nine

Shay didn't hesitate. "Think again. It's a lousy idea."

He blinked, surprise widening his eyes. "Why?"

"Did you ever stop to think that I might not like to have my picture taken?"

He didn't buy that. "Why not? You're a beautiful woman."

"I don't want to see my face anywhere except in the mirror. You of all people should understand someone wanting to preserve her privacy," she said.

"I also understand the need for self-promotion. You can't expect to expand your career if you don't get some kind of publicity. This advertising promotion could give you more work than you can handle."

"I already have more work than I can handle."

He rapped his fingers impatiently against the steering wheel. This wasn't going the way he thought it would. "You said something yesterday after I signed an autograph for the deputy, something about playing the game. You said you weren't referring to football but the game of being a celebrity. You made it sound as though you've had firsthand experience. Evidently, you didn't enjoy it. It doesn't have to be that way."

"I'm not willing to pay the price of living in a goldfish bowl being watched and judged. Quincy brought me to Cadance to get away from all that."

"Quincy told me he brought you here when you were six years old. That's a young age for someone to have a negative opinion about publicity."

"Not if the publicity happens to be about the six-year-old's mother."

"Your mother?" For a few seconds he simply stared at her as he searched his mind for a clue as to who her mother was. "You said your mother's name is Monica Sutton? No offense, but I never heard of her."

"She's probably never heard of Dillon Street, either. Unless you watch soap operas and game shows during the day, you wouldn't know her. She plays a lovable ditsy owner of a flower shop in a daytime soap called 'Rose Red' and appears regularly in the center square of a popular daytime game show. She likes to refer to herself as a television personality rather than an actress. She thrives on the cameras, the reporters, the attention."

"But you don't."

"No, I don't, but it's her life, not mine."

Dillon grinned suddenly.

"What's so funny?" she asked with a slight edge in her voice.

"I'm trying to picture Quincy married to a soap opera star."

Shay decided to tell Dillon the truth now rather than later. If he was going to have a problem with her illegitimacy, it was better that she find that out now. "He wasn't."

Dillon blinked and stared. "Wasn't what? Married to a soap opera star? You just said—"

"I never said my parents were married. My mother phoned Quincy when I was six and asked him to come out to Los Angeles to get me. Up until that phone call, he hadn't even known he had a child. He brought me back here, and except for occasional vacations with Monica and going to college, I've lived with him."

Straddling the seat, Dillon turned so he could face her. "The waitress at Murray's Café mentioned your mother. Was she from around here?"

"My mother, Doris and Quincy all went to school together. Monica and Quincy were high school sweethearts until Monica decided she wanted to be somebody other than a wife and mother like all her friends planned to be. Quincy was perfectly content living in Cadance, and they broke up. A few weeks later Monica left for Hollywood and fame and fortune."

"And she found it."

Shay nodded. "Along with four husbands. I got the impression during our last phone call that number five might be standing in the wings."

Dillon tilted his head to one side and studied her expression carefully. "Is your parents' marital status the reason you don't want publicity?"

"Partly," she admitted. "It wouldn't make as much difference to me as it would to her. Monica doesn't need her illegitimate daughter talking to curious reporters who prefer juicy news over dry facts. I wouldn't volunteer the information, but that doesn't mean an enterprising journalist wouldn't dig around and come up with Monica's past history. Most of the older people in Cadance know Monica's real history and would probably be willing to talk about it. It's one of the few naughty tidbits Cadance can brag about."

"You don't want publicity so you can protect your mother from having her past dredged up?"

Shay nodded. "She has a reputation for being everybody's best friend, for being squeaky clean. Having an illegitimate child would definitely put an end to her image and possibly end her career."

"Maybe not. Fans are more tolerant than you think. But it might not come to that. The photo layout is a one-shot deal. Your name and hers are different. She won't be linked to you if that's what you want."

"I still don't want to take part in any publicity scheme." Something in his eyes made her ask, "You've already made the arrangements, haven't you?"

"I made a phone call this morning to my office in San Francisco. My secretary is putting a couple of staff members on it and will call back once the arrangements are finalized. The idea is to show the designers in their own surroundings, to see where and how they work, the person behind the designs they create." He added, "Amy likes the idea. So did your father when I told him about it. He doesn't seem to have the same fears about the past coming out that you do."

Shay argued. "I don't have any problems with the concept. The idea is a publicist's dream. I just want to be left out of it." She turned to face the bow. "We don't need to continue this lesson. You've mastered the boat well enough to get to my place if there's an emergency."

Dillon didn't change his position. "I want you included in this publicity, Shay. I'll make sure the person interviewing you stays away from your personal life. No one has to know who your parents are if that's the way you want it."

"That's the way it has to be. Monica's career means everything to her, and I don't want to be responsible for making trouble for her. Her career is her life."

Dillon didn't think much of a woman who would think more of her career than her own child. "Is that why she sent for Quincy to come after you? So no one would know she had a child?"

Shay heard the censure in his voice and realized she'd given him the wrong impression. "Giving me up was more for my sake than for hers. It wasn't easy for her before or after I was born. She supported us by working two, sometimes three jobs and a few bit parts here and there. When she got her first break, she'd also met the man who was eventually her first husband."

"Was he the reason she called Quincy? Her new husband didn't want an instant family?"

She shook her head. "One night she was giving a party to celebrate a new part in a sitcom, and one of the party-goers who'd had too much to drink had wandered into my bedroom. Monica found him passed out across the foot of my bed. To protect me from something worse than a drunk, she called Quincy."

"She could have changed her life-style. Having a career in show business doesn't require attending parties and exposing one's family to drunks and worse. That was her choice."

Shay stiffened suddenly as a clanging sound carried across the water.

"What's that?" asked Dillon.

"Quincy wants us to come in." She leaned over and hit the center of the steering wheel twice. The horn blared in two short blasts. "Now he knows we heard him and that we're returning."

Dillon started the engine and headed the boat back to Quincy's dock. Timing was as vital in this situation as it had been on the football field, Dillon mused. He would back down on the publicity angle for now. But not on their involvement with each other. Their time would come. And soon.

His inexperience in handling a boat was obvious when he cut the engine too soon as they neared the dock. Shay used the time to step over the windshield and walk out on the bow of the boat with the line in her hand as they slowly coasted forward. She had time to glance up at the cabin and to see Quincy in his wheelchair near the large bell he'd rigged up years ago to summon her in off the lake. This was the first time since his accident that he'd voluntarily ventured outside on his own, as far as she knew. The ramp had been her idea and she'd had it built after finding out how serious and permanent his injuries were. He had refused to use it.

Once the boat was finally secured, Shay walked beside Dillon up the ramp to where Quincy was waiting for them.

Quincy had a message for Dillon. "Sorry to interrupt the lesson, but your friend Flynn called. He said it's important that he talk to you as soon as possible."

Dillon nodded and left Shay's side to enter the cabin.

Shay started to turn back to go to the boat when her father called her back. "Shay? Don't leave just yet. There's something I want to say."

She looked at him but kept the distance between them. With a light laugh that contained little humor, she said, "I think that's the problem, Quincy. We both said too much the other night and are having trouble getting past the things we heard. Maybe we should leave it alone."

He shook his head. "We have to get past it, Shay."

She bit her lip. She wanted to make peace with her father but was concerned that they might end up rehashing the previous arguments.

He took her silence as her willingness to mend the break in their relationship. "You pointed out my attitude needed work and you were right. I have been feeling sorry for myself since the accident and have been too dependent on you. I shouldn't have thrown the past at you, making it sound as if you owed me for taking you away from that unhealthy environment in Los Angeles. I haven't ever told you, but I've never once regretted bringing you here."

This time Shay met him halfway. Stepping over to a bench near his chair, she sat down. "I have been treating you like a helpless child as you said I have. I only recently realized I was enjoying being needed, being able to pay you back a little."

"For what?" he asked, clearly surprised by her comment.

"For raising me when you could have turned Monica down." She smiled faintly at his shocked look. "The fine citizens of Cadance have long memories and occasionally I've been reminded how lucky I am you took me in. I'm the pathetic innocent child, you're a saint, and Monica is the sinner in the eyes of the town."

Quincy muttered a couple of unsavory words under his breath. "What our neighbors have conveniently forgotten is how wild I was before I brought you back from Los Angeles. Having the responsibility of a small child made me grow up fast. I've never had a single regret about having you with me. Don't ever let anyone ever tell you differently."

"I never thought you did." It was her turn to be surprised.

"But you did say helping me through this was a way of paying me back for raising you. I never wanted payment or pats on the back or eternal gratitude, Shay. All I want is for you to be happy, not to wear yourself out looking after me. That's why I was angry. You were hurting yourself by helping me." He paused, then jerked his head in the direction of the doorway Dillon had disappeared into. "However, if you let this guy go, I might get angry all over again."

Shay didn't bother pretending not to know what he was talking about. "I've only known him for two days, Quincy. We barely know each other."

"Sometimes one day is enough."

Suddenly restless, Shay got to her feet. "He'll be leaving for San Francisco soon. It won't be a case of me letting him go. He'll be going all on his own."

"Did you stop to think that sometimes a woman needs to give a man a good reason to stick around?"

"He has one, remember? Some nut is threatening him and blowing up his car. As soon as the guy is stopped from harassing Dillon, it will be safe for him to go home.''

''That's not what I meant.''

''I know,'' she said, sighing heavily. ''Leave it alone, Quincy.''

''You aren't going to tell me you aren't attracted to the man, are you? There is nothing wrong with my eyes, you know. I see how you try hard not to look at him and even harder not to touch him.''

Shay suddenly realized she and her father were no longer alone. Dillon was standing on the other side of the screen door, his gaze riveted on Shay's face. She knew he had heard Quincy's question and was waiting to hear her answer.

Quincy was looking out over the water. Shay directed her gaze at Dillon briefly so he knew she was aware he was there. ''Just because I'm attracted to him doesn't mean I'm going to do anything about it. I don't like crowds.''

''Crowds?'' asked Quincy with a puzzled frown as he brought his attention back to her. ''What crowds?''

''Your temporary roommate has an active social life in San Francisco,'' she said, clearly for Dillon's benefit. ''He's going to want to get back to it. You've said yourself that Cadance falls asleep when the sun sets.''

Even through the gray mesh screen, Shay could see Dillon's eyes narrow, his jaw clench. He opened the door and let it slam closed behind him as he stepped out onto the deck.

Quincy looked up. ''Everything all right?''

"They could be better," he drawled.

Shay met his gaze. The dry amusement in his voice was not reflected in his eyes as he stared back at her. He was angry.

Unsatisfied with Dillon's reply, Quincy asked, "Your friend sounded as though it was urgent you contact him. Have there been more threats?"

"Indirectly." Dillon sat down on the bench next to Shay. "Someone broke into my office at Good Sports and riffled my secretary's desk. Some of her computer disks are missing, her Rolodex, and a number of files."

"Someone's trying to find out where you are," murmured Quincy.

"It looks that way."

"Is there any chance he was successful?"

"Beryl didn't write down my location. The only thing Flynn is concerned about is that the arrangements made with the photographer were jotted down on Beryl's daily calendar. Since Shay was scheduled to be the first designer photographed, an address might have been listed."

"Why is your secretary handling the publicity arrangements for Dream Street?"

"I know the photographer. He was more apt to do a favor for me than he would for Amy. We're asking him to work us into an already busy schedule."

"Which address did you give your secretary?" She had a feeling she knew but she asked anyway.

"Quincy's."

"Damn it, Dillon!"

"Shay," he said patiently. "Your lane has more pits than a coal mine. Your father's cabin is easier to find and to get to without jarring a few teeth loose. The guy won't connect me with the Dream Street advertisement arrangements. My secretary can't remember exactly what she wrote, but she is sure she didn't write anything down that would indicate I was personally involved in the shoot. Her appointment calendar is missing, so she can't check her entry."

Shay had heard enough. Standing, she planted her hands on her hips and glared at Dillon. "You promised Quincy wouldn't be in any danger from the guy who is after you if you stayed here. This man is obviously determined to find you if he's tearing apart your office. I don't want Quincy in danger if this lunatic shows up here."

"I understand your concerns, Shay," he said with forced patience. "We've taken every precaution to prevent anyone from knowing where I am. But if he did come looking for me, I'd rather be here than leave you and Quincy to deal with him alone."

Quincy nodded. "Let him come. Now that we know there's a possibility he might pay us a visit, we have time to arrange for a reception committee. It will be a good way to trap him and end this harassment."

Shay looked at her father with impatience. "This isn't a game of poker, Quincy. If this guy shows up, what's to stop him from setting off a bomb to blow up this cabin while you and Dillon are inside?" The familiar look of resentment crossed Quincy's face, and she reacted to it. "I know you think I'm treating you like a child again, but I'd be concerned even if you didn't have any physical problems. The fleetest track star can't outrun a bomb."

"You're worrying about something that will likely never happen," Quincy said with a hint of irritation. "You heard Dillon. The chances of this lunatic finding him are slim."

"But not impossible," she insisted. She turned to Dillon. "I don't think it's fair of you to expose Quincy to danger. That wasn't part of our deal."

She was about to say more when Dillon closed his fingers around her upper arm and drew her close to him as he stood.

"Would you excuse us, Quincy?"

The older man was clearly surprised by the request. "I guess so," he murmured, his gaze darting to Shay's rebellious expression.

Dillon pulled Shay with him down the ramp and toward the dock, his grip on her arm as stiff as his expression. He didn't stop until they were standing on the dock next to her boat.

"What in hell are you trying to do to him, Shay?" he asked in a voice laced with steel. "Unman him completely?"

"I'm trying to protect him. You certainly aren't. You have no right putting him in danger like this."

"He's where he wants to be, doing what he wants to do, living his life as a cop and a man, not an invalid.

You admitted he's been more alive the last couple of days than he has since the accident. Now you want to seal him away in a sterile environment again just when he's beginning to breathe fresh air. He's a man, not a hothouse orchid.''

Shay jerked her arm away from his firm hold. Taking a step back, she said angrily, ''He's also all I have.''

Dillon's anger evaporated. ''Shay.''

She shook her head and turned away to untie the stern line. She couldn't fight them both. Holding the bow line she'd just loosened, she stepped into the boat. ''Maybe you would understand how I feel if the person in danger was your sister instead of my father.''

''I'll make sure nothing happens to your father, Shay,'' he said quietly. ''You're going to have to trust me.''

''What about you?''

Puzzled, he asked, ''What about me?''

''Can you promise nothing will happen to you, either?''

''You know I can't do that.''

''Has it occurred to you I might be concerned about you, too?'' When her question was met with a blank stare, she added, ''No, I can see it hasn't. I would be devastated if I lost either you or Quincy to this madman.''

Stunned by the emotion in her voice, he reached for her, but she pushed the boat away from the dock with her foot, widening the gap between them.

Shay turned her back on him and moved to the helm to start the engine. The throaty sound of the engine throbbing to life made further conversation impossible even if Dillon could have thought of anything to say. Shay didn't look back as she pushed the throttle to full power and left the dock and Dillon quickly behind her.

Dillon stared after her for a few minutes, then turned back toward Quincy's cabin. The older man hadn't moved from his position on the deck. By the dark frown on his face, he wasn't happy about the quick exit Shay had made.

"It's not possible for Shay to understand how a man thinks when there's a threat of danger," explained Quincy. "Her instinct is to protect the people she cares about, where you and I prefer to stand our ground and fight."

Dillon sat back down on the bench. Stretching his long legs out on the deck, he leaned against the railing behind him, his gaze on the boat growing smaller in the distance.

"She was right about one thing," murmured Dillon. "I shouldn't have involved you and her in this. I honestly didn't think this guy could find me here. If I thought it would keep my enemy away from here, I'd leave right now. But if he finds out I'm here, he'll come looking for me. I don't want either you or Shay to have your hospitality returned with violence."

Quincy smiled faintly. "One thing I've learned from this accident is wanting something doesn't mean we can always get it, no matter how badly we want it."

"I'm learning that lesson since I met your daughter."

Quincy's smile became almost smug. "She'll come around once she realizes we can take care of this character who's hounding you." Tilting his head slightly to one side, Quincy asked, "How is your friend's investigation going about finding out who has a grudge against you?"

"He has a couple of suspects in mind. One is a guy who played football on an opposing team when I was playing. He happens to be the one responsible for injuring my knee and ending my career."

"Why would this man have it in for you? He ruined your career. You didn't end his."

"In a roundabout way, I did. He'd been on team probation for previous infractions of the rules. The videotape of the game when I was injured showed clearly that he not only intentionally tripped me but brought his knee down on my leg after I was down. When I was in the hospital, I found out he'd got thrown off the team. No other team picked up his option. He was through permanently. Jordan Reinhold blamed me instead of himself."

"If it is him, why would he wait all this time to get his twisted revenge?"

"Flynn's looking into it. He thinks one reason might be that the announcements of the nominations for the Hall of Fame were made public last month, and I was on the list. Reinhold wasn't. If he's having personal or business problems, he could be blaming me for all the bad luck he's having in his life. He's the type to shift the responsibility of something going wrong to someone else. Flynn's investigating.''

''What about the other suspect?''

''He's an ex-husband of a woman I dated briefly. He's the jealous type and even though they're divorced, he feels possessive about his ex-wife. I've run into him a couple of times in restaurants and he's tried to start something, even though I haven't seen his ex-wife in months.''

They both heard the phone ringing. Dillon stood immediately. ''Do you mind if I answer that? Flynn had another call while he was talking to me and was supposed to call me back.''

''Go ahead.''

By the time Dillon had finished his conversation with his friend, Quincy had pushed his wheelchair into the living room.

''Well?'' the older man asked when he saw Dillon's hard expression.

''Shay's really going to love this,'' murmured Dillon as he rubbed a hand across the back of his neck.

''Why? What's happening?''

''Flynn's operative who was tailing Reinhold reported he boarded a plane. His destination was Minneapolis. It looks like we're going to have company, after all.''

Chapter Ten

The only light illuminating Shay's kitchen was the one above the sink, assisted by the occasional flash of lightning followed by rumbles of thunder that accompanied the downpour of rain pelting the windows. She was able to see what she was doing without having to turn on the bright strips of fluorescent tubing overhead.

The front of Shay's white batiste nightgown was damp and clinging from the rain that had blown in through the windows before she'd been able to get them closed. The nearly transparent fabric clung to her breasts, and felt cold and clammy against her skin. The way her fingers ached, she would have had difficulty undoing the buttons down the front of the nightgown to remove it. Soaking her hands in a bowl of ice water was more urgent than changing into a dry gown. The cold water was beginning to ease the painful cramping in her fingers caused from sewing for more than ten hours straight.

Having only herself to blame for the pain didn't help. Instead of pacing herself, she had plied her needle with a vengeance, trying to do two weeks' work in one day. She bit her lip as the frigid cold penetrated her skin. She sighed heavily. She was such an idiot.

She didn't realize she'd spoken aloud until she heard Dillon's quiet voice behind her saying, "You're not the only one."

Whirling her head around, she saw he was really there and not a figment of her imagination. His legs were slightly parted, his hands on his hips. The light above the sink didn't extend far across the room, but she could make out his shadowy figure filling the doorway between the kitchen and the dark dining room.

"Good Lord, Dillon. You nearly gave me a heart attack."

"Sorry. Your door was unlocked so I walked in. I figured you wouldn't hear me over the loud sound effects going on outside so I didn't bother knocking." He stepped closer, his gaze on the sink. "What are you doing?"

She noticed his hair, shirt and jeans were wet. "You didn't come across the lake in this storm, did you? Please tell me you didn't do anything that stupid."

"I certainly didn't drive over. One roller-coaster ride down your lane was enough, thank you. I took your father's boat, and you'll be pleased to know I parked it without any damage to either your boat or his or the dock."

"Docked the boat," she corrected out of habit.

"That's what I said."

"You said 'parked.' You don't park a boat. You park a car." She shook her head to negate the conversation. "Never mind, we're getting off the subject of your being on the lake during a storm at midnight."

"I'm here, aren't I? The boat and I are both in one piece, so what are you upset about?"

"I can't believe you would be foolish enough to take the boat out on the lake during a thunderstorm after having only one lesson. Do you have any idea how dangerous that is?"

He took a few steps into the kitchen. "I did get the general impression nature was not exactly helping me, especially with the wind whipping the waves and lightning flashing across the sky. You never answered my question. What are you doing at the sink?"

Grabbing a towel, she began to dry her hands, concealing her abused fingers. "It's nothing. I'd rather talk about why you would risk coming across the lake during a storm. Is Quincy all right?"

"Quincy is fine. He was tired after all the unaccustomed exercise he had today and went to bed early. I told him I was coming over here. He'll call on the two-way radio if he needs anything. But I don't think he'll need to. He was asleep when I left." Dillon had closed the distance between them and looked down into the sink. He sucked in his breath when he saw the pink-tinged water and the melting cubes of ice in the white ceramic bowl sitting in the sink.

"What in hell have you done?" He moved toward her. "Did you cut yourself?"

Shay stepped back. "If you made the trip over here just to yell at me, you can turn around and go back to Quincy's, storm or no storm," she said defensively. "I'm not in the mood to argue with you." When he ignored her and began to remove the towel from her hands, she protested, "You are the most arrogant, stubborn man I have ever had the misfortune to meet. Leave the towel alone. My hands are still wet."

Ignoring her protests, he tossed the towel onto the counter. He turned her hands over and examined the reddened tips and the multitude of small bluish nicks, which had been deep enough to bleed where she'd obviously pricked them with a needle or straight pin.

"What in hell are you trying to prove?"

"I worked longer than I should have, that's all." Her anger vanished when she heard his voice catch as though her pain hurt him. "You heard me when you came in. I called myself an idiot. I should have known better."

His voice was low and serious. "I'm an even bigger fool than you are. I've been chopping wood for your father most of the afternoon to try to work off my need for you. Aside from a healthy stack of firewood, I managed to get two slivers, drop a heavy log on my foot, and nearly take off a couple of toes with the ax. You've spent your time abusing your hands sewing as though your life depended on it. It looks like neither of us would get any awards for intelligence today."

"I guess not."

"We both know why we are accidents waiting to happen. Our minds have been on something else besides what we were doing. Working ourselves into the ground isn't the answer."

She bent her head to look down at their clasped hands. He was holding her fingers so gently, she felt her throat tighten with emotion. She didn't try to pull away. Slowly raising her head, she met his gaze, her breath hitching when she saw the heated expression in the depths of his eyes.

"You've come here tonight to end the waiting, haven't you?"

Raising her hands to his mouth, he brushed his tongue over her mistreated fingers, his eyes dark with a naked hunger as he held her gaze captive.

"Not an ending, Shay," he said softly. "A beginning. I know you would be more comfortable if we'd followed the conventional route of dating, spending time together, getting to know each other." He ran the back of a finger down the side of her neck, pleased to feel her pulse accelerate. "It wouldn't make a difference. I can't imagine wanting you any more than I do right now or less than I did the first moment I saw you."

A crack of thunder vibrated through the cabin, a fitting punctuation to Dillon's statement. The air around them sizzled with a current so powerful and emotionally charged, they were both trembling.

Dillon released one of her hands and trailed his fingers down the front of her nightgown where the damp cloth clung to her feminine curves. Only the thin wet fabric separated his hand from her bare breasts as he closed his hand over one luscious mound. His smile was full of sensual satisfaction as he felt her nipple harden against his palm.

His voice was husky with suppressed desire. "You might as well be naked."

When he replaced his hand with his mouth, Shay made a groan deep in her throat and let her head fall back, her fingers curling into his hair to hold him against her.

Dillon's senses began to spin as he heard the soft yearning sounds his intimate caresses were drawing from her.

No woman had ever brought him to the brink of exploding so quickly, so powerfully. And he hadn't even kissed her. Pressed against him, she felt like the fantasy he had often dreamed of and had never found. Until now. Her taste went to his head like the finest Irish whiskey, intoxicating him until he was drunk on the scent of her skin.

"I won't let anything happen to you or your father, Shay," he murmured. "Trust me. I won't let you down."

"I trust you. I don't trust the man who's trying to hurt you."

Every touch, every stroke, satisfied that moment's craving, but he needed her more than his next breath.

Raising his head, he spoke only inches away from her parted lips. Her breathing was fast and warm against his mouth. "Kiss me, Shay. Show me you want me, too."

Her arms slid up his chest to wrap around his neck. She raised up on her toes and covered his mouth as though she was starving for the sustenance she knew only he could provide.

The storm outside was equaled in intensity to the primitive writhing desire coiling through them. Like the outside elements, the current of passion was demanding, urgent, and out of their control. Thunder in their blood throbbed. Need like hot rain flowed through their veins.

Unable to resist the temptation of her warm body, Dillon gathered the material of her gown in his fists until he found her bare thighs. The thin cord of control restraining him nearly snapped when he realized nothing separated him from her damp heat. He lifted her onto the bare table and ran his hands over her thighs. She trembled when he placed his hands on her knees and spread them apart enough for him to step between them.

The scent of her perfume drifted up to him, and his body clenched violently. Long days and longer nights of wanting this woman had his control stretched to the limit. He pushed the limits farther by stroking her firm, smooth thighs.

The sound she made deep in her throat when his fingers found her moist center was nearly his undoing. She cried out and clutched his shoulders when he stroked her intimately, her fingernails leaving marks of passion on his skin. He shuddered violently, his body aching with the need to bury himself deep inside her.

He'd wanted to take his time, wanted to make them both crazy with desire, to make this first time unforgettable for her. Lord knows, he wouldn't forget a single moment.

With his hands at her waist, he wrapped her legs around his hips and hoisted her off the table. Her arms encircled his neck, and she held on tightly.

"Don't let go," he said in a voice hoarse with hunger. "Hold me or I'll shatter into a million pieces."

Holding her intimately close to him as he took her up the stairs had him shaking with the need to end the tension spiraling through every cell of his body. With every step, her body rubbed against his taut arousal. He took her mouth with a desperate hunger, groaning against her lips.

Finally reaching her bedroom, Dillon nudged the door open farther with his foot and carried her over to her bed. For a moment he simply held her in his arms, his gaze locked with hers. He slid his hands down to cup her buttocks to hold her firmly against his throbbing loins. It was torture, pure, refined torture. And he didn't want it to end.

"Are you sure this is what you want, Shay? If you have any doubts, tell me now."

"No doubts, no regrets, no recriminations. I want this as badly as you do. Maybe more."

He smiled faintly. "I don't think that's possible." Referring to her earlier remark to her father about his reputation, he added, "There are no crowds here, Shay. This is between you and me. Nothing and no one has ever made me feel like this, as though I'm going to shatter and only you can put me together again."

Shay didn't want to talk. She was overwhelmed by myriad feelings too vast to be labeled. Only felt. Tightening her arms around his neck, she raised her body against his, slowly lowering her hips to stroke over the hard ridge of his arousal. She whimpered softly, closing her eyes to absorb the primitive erotic desire surging through her body.

He groaned her name but made no move to lower her onto the bed.

"What are you waiting for?" she asked in a breathless whisper.

"You," he said hoarsely. "I've been waiting for you for a long time and didn't even know it."

Lowering her onto the turquoise spread, Dillon followed her down, unable to be apart from her even long enough to remove his clothing. His hands swept over her, sliding the damp gown off her shoulders, torturing himself with a slow drawing down of the fabric over her breasts, her waist, her hips. Finally he tugged the Lady Shay creation off completely and tossed it away.

Shay was in a rush to experience every nuance of lovemaking in Dillon's arms. She didn't feel the soreness in her fingers as she worked the buttons of his shirt loose and slid her hands inside the opening. Her sensitized fingertips smoothed over his chest. His body was strong and hard. Her touch was demanding, yet gentle.

A small part of her mind still capable of rational thought knew that this was right. Making love with him might not be wise but for this moment, it was all she wanted. He was all she wanted.

"Dillon," she breathed, yearning and desire making her voice shake.

Somehow he managed to remove his own clothing, and Shay gasped when she felt the burning heat of his naked flesh against her body. Her hands caressed and stroked and discovered taut muscles, and she heard him murmur her name in response, his breathing ragged and fragmented. She found herself amazed that she was able to give him similar incendiary sensations to the ones he was giving her.

He took her mouth almost desperately, and Shay felt the world spin. Then she realized he had rolled onto his back, taking her with him until she was lying on top of his strong body.

Her hair fell forward, and she brought a hand up to pull it back out of the way over her shoulder.

"No." He took her hand away. "Leave it."

Dillon's hands went to her hips, his gaze fixed on her face. "Shay," he murmured thickly.

"Yes." Her hands clasped his shoulders. "Now."

Her breathing stuttered to a halt when she felt his fingers on her soft inner thighs, parting her legs with gentle pressure.

"You feel so good," he said huskily. His hands clasped her hips, positioning her. "So damn good." As he began to enter her, he saw her lashes lower. "Don't close your eyes. Let me see how I make you feel when I'm inside you."

When he raised his hips and brought them together, a crack of lightning slashed down from the sky and thunder crashed loudly outside the bedroom window, rattling the glass. The storm outside was a mere spring breeze compared to the intensity inside the bedroom.

Shay was mesmerized by the look of fevered desire in his eyes as he began to move, controlling her with his hands on her hips until she took over on her own. Time took on a different tempo. Seconds seemed longer than minutes. Minutes were like hours as they sought an end to the spiraling tension holding them prisoner. Yet time seemed to spin by.

It suddenly seemed vitally important to Shay that Dillon knew who he was making love with. "Say my name."

His dark eyes held hers as he slipped a hand between them. He said her name clearly. "Lady Shay." Then he touched her intimately, setting off a reaction that catapulted them both over the edge of sanity and into a world of satisfaction.

He murmured her name again as he held her close. She collapsed on his chest, her body trembling with the aftershocks caused by their tumultuous lovemaking. Dillon closed his eyes and breathed in her scent, his body shaking as though he had a fever.

Gradually their breathing slowed, and with it, realization that everything had changed, not only in their relationship but in every aspect of their lives. Neither would be the same as they'd been before.

For the first time in memory Dillon was insecure with a woman. She was attracted to him physically, but he wanted more from her. He wanted everything she could give. As he ran his hand slowly down her spine, he realized no woman had ever mattered this much to him.

He was in love with her.

He closed his eyes and tightened his arms around Shay as though she would disappear if he didn't hold on to her. He loosened his hold slightly when it occurred to him that the bonds he needed to forge were emotional as well as physical.

"Shay?" he murmured against her throat.

"Hmm?"

"Are you all right? I didn't hurt you, did I?"

She raised her head and looked down at him, her eyes wide with astonishment. "You didn't hurt me." That would come later, after he returned to San Francisco, she thought. She lowered her lashes to hide her expression from him.

He felt her withdraw from him even though they were still intimately joined. How could that be? he wondered. He rolled with her until she was lying on her back.

Looking down at her, he demanded softly, "Look at me, Shay. Talk to me. I want to know what you're thinking."

Slowly, Shay raised her lashes and met his dark gaze. She didn't want to talk. Then she would have to think. All she wanted was to lose herself in the magic they created together. She lifted her hips slightly, feeling his automatic response as he hardened inside her. "Don't talk. Not now. Later."

Dillon groaned at the husky tone in her voice. She moved again, and he forgot everything except how she made him feel.

Shay felt as though she'd only just closed her eyes when she heard Dillon call her name. Barely awake, she frowned. His voice sounded distant instead of softly sensuous. Dragging her eyes open, she expected to find him in the bed next to her, but she saw only an indentation in the pillow and an empty space.

Leaning on an elbow, she searched the room. Since her bedroom was small, the search didn't take long. Understanding what she was seeing was going to take a while.

He was standing in front of her closet, impatiently shoving hangers back and forth on the rod.

He was fully dressed.

"Dillon?" Her voice croaked like a drowsy frog. Clearing her throat, she asked, "What are you doing?"

"Packing some clothes for you."

She sighed heavily, feeling let down by his morning-after manners, which definitely needed work.

"I thought we'd already settled this. I'm not going to the grand opening in Minneapolis." Tilting her head to one side, she asked, "Did you think I would change my mind once we became lovers?"

"We aren't going to Minneapolis," he told her as he chose another shirt to add to the pile over one arm.

Shay brushed her tangled hair away from her face, wishing she could wipe away her confusion that easily. She wasn't all that familiar with proper behavior between lovers after spending the night together for the first time. This wasn't even close to what she expected.

Maybe she was still asleep and this was all a bad dream. Pinching her forearm, she muttered, "Ouch!"

Dillon approached the bed with an armload of clothing. "What's the matter?"

If she had a pencil and paper handy, she could have made a very long list. "I thought I would test myself to see if I was still asleep. Guess what? I'm awake. What happened between falling into an exhausted sleep in your arms and waking up to find you going through my closet?"

Dillon dropped the clothing onto the end of the bed and sat down on the edge of the mattress near her hip. "This isn't how I wanted our first morning together to be, either, sweetheart." He leaned down and kissed her, taking his time savoring her mouth. Then he made a disgruntled sound that was pure frustration, followed by a muttered curse. "You've got time for a shower if you make it quick. I told Flynn we'd be at your father's as soon as possible."

Grabbing the sheet in both hands, she held it to her breasts and sat up. "Flynn? Your friend Flynn? The private investigator Flynn? When did you talk to him? How did you talk to him?"

"Quincy called on the radio while I was downstairs trying to find your coffee grounds. The canister is empty."

"Coffee is in the canister marked Flour."

"Of course. Why didn't I think of that?" he asked with dry sarcasm.

"The canister marked Coffee is too small, so I use the larger one."

"Shay," he murmured with a tinge of humor. "I'm not that interested in the subject of canisters."

"You brought it up."

"Well, now I'm getting rid of it. We have more important things to talk about. Flynn called Quincy from a pay phone in Cadance to get directions to your father's cabin. That's where he thought I'd be."

The obvious urgency behind Flynn's unexpected visit overcame any girlish blushes that might have been triggered by her father and Flynn knowing Dillon had spent the night with her.

"What's happened?"

Dillon took her hand and held it securely between his. "The photographer my secretary had arranged to do the publicity shots was contacted by a man who said he was from one of the high-profile magazines. He was supposedly interested in covering the story on the different designers who create fantasy and romance with a needle and thread. It didn't occur to the photographer to ask how the journalist knew about the project."

"Do you think the journalist is your mad bomber?"

"We can't take the chance that he's not. The photographer didn't know he wasn't supposed to talk about the shoot for Dream Street and gave the so-called journalist the name of the designer he was going to photograph first and where she lived. That's you and the address is Quincy's."

"You said neither your secretary nor Flynn would have told anyone where you went. Why would this guy connect your absence with me?"

"I'm guessing he came across the photographer's name and yours on Beryl's desk calendar. He might just be grasping at straws. Since the proposed advertising is for my sister's business, yet on my secretary's calendar, he might make the assumption I'm taking a personal interest in this particular designer. One of Flynn's men tracked the guy to the airport in Minneapolis where he rented a car. That was yesterday. That's why you and I are leaving the area. I don't want him even in the same state with you."

Shay stared at him as he returned to her closet and hauled out a suitcase from the top shelf. "I can't leave Quincy, Dillon."

"Your father is taken care of." He set the case on the bed and flipped open the lid. "You might want to pack your own things rather than leave it up to me. I might leave out some essential bit of feminine stuff you need."

"Wait a minute," she protested. Tugging the sheet off the bed, she wrapped it around her like a sarong as she stood. "As usual, you're charging ahead at full steam and I haven't even taken the first step."

"We'll have plenty of time later to go over every little complaint you have when we're in the air."

"In the air? Like flying-in-an-airplane type of 'in the air'?"

He raised a brow. "I don't have a flying carpet handy. Of course I mean in an airplane. You're wasting valuable time, sweetheart. We really need to get going. I'll round up the hounds so we can take them with us while you pack enough clothes for a couple of days. Your father and Dugan can take care of the dogs while we're gone.''

"Who's Dugan?'' she asked weakly on the off chance she'd get a straight answer.

"You'll meet him when we get to your father's cabin. He arrived with Flynn.''

"Flynn is here?''

"He'll be at your father's cabin when we get there.'' He took her by the shoulders, turned her around, and shoved her toward the bathroom door. "Go take your shower, Shay. We're running out of time.''

Standing under the shower a few minutes later, Shay lifted her face to receive the full brunt of the spray. The way to deal with steamrollers, she decided, was to go in the same direction or get flattened. She didn't need to question Dillon's reasons for wanting to put some distance between himself and his enemy. This guy had already proved his intentions were serious. But she didn't understand why Dillon was insisting she leave with him. She couldn't see how she was in any danger. Dillon was the one needing protection.

As she toweled off and dressed in a pair of black slacks and an ivory shirt, she could finally admit to herself she would do whatever it took to keep Dillon safe. Dillon's enemy would expect him to be traveling alone. If being with Dillon protected him for a short time, if that meant leaving with him for however long it took, then that's what she'd do. As long as Quincy was all right. Which evidently is where the person named Dugan came in.

Dillon had found another suitcase in the meantime and had filled it and the other one with enough clothing for a month. Thanks to her experience traveling with her mother two weeks every summer, Shay had learned the fine art of packing light. Closing one suitcase after quickly repacking it, she instructed Dillon to put the other case away. She wasn't going to take every item of clothing she owned.

He had stood patiently near the bed while she repacked, but protested when she proceeded to make the bed.

"Shay, we don't have time for you to tidy the whole damn cabin before we go."

"Sorry," she murmured. "Habit. Why don't you take my case with you in Quincy's boat and I'll get the dogs out of the shed. They'll travel better with me. I'll meet you at Quincy's."

Dillon nodded in agreement, took two steps toward the door, then came back to her. Sliding his hand around the back of her neck, he kissed her. For a man who had just said he was in a hurry, he took his time, raising his head when her breathing became ragged.

"I hate this guy for making our first time together seem like a rushed one-night stand. Last night meant more to me than that. Don't forget that, no matter what happens today."

She lifted her hand to his unshaven jaw. "I'll remember everything about last night."

Dillon kissed her again, unsatisfied with her answer. He would like to have had more time to convince her their relationship was only starting, not ending. Dillon realized he could use some reassurance from her. He knew she cared for him but had no idea how much. He knew her well enough by now to know she would never have gone to bed with him unless she felt more than a fleeting attraction.

But the clock was ticking, and he didn't have time to clear up any doubts or misconceptions. He hated the feeling of having left things unsettled between him and Shay, yet he didn't have a choice.

Once the mess with his enemy was over, they would have all the time in the world. Perhaps forever.

Chapter Eleven

The moment Shay brought the boat alongside Quincy's dock, the three dogs jumped out and ran toward the cabin. She'd had the devil's own sweet time getting the dogs into the boat. They had wanted to play. Shay would get two in the boat with only one left to coax aboard. When she got the last one in, the other two would hop out of the boat. It had taken her longer than Dillon probably expected, but three dogs weren't easy to handle. About halfway to the cabin, the dogs planted their paws into the grass and began their gritty chorus of displeasure.

As Shay secured the boat to the dock, she glanced up at the deck to see what had set the dogs off. Since the dogs had been at Quincy's hundreds of times in the past and they now tolerated Dillon, that left the two strangers on the deck with Quincy and Dillon. Along with skunks and baths, the dogs disliked strangers.

She whistled and the dogs quieted but remained alert to any sudden moves by the two men who were standing near the rail facing the lake. As she walked across the stretch of grass between the lake and the cabin, Shay guessed that the tall, lean man standing next to Dillon was his friend Flynn.

Whoever he was, the man was studying her with the same intensity she was directing toward him. He was dressed all in black from his Western-style boots to his jeans and his shirt. All he needed was a cowboy hat, a set of spurs, and a sheriff's badge, she thought, to complete the picture of a lawman from the previous century. Or a cattle rustler. The villains were usually the ones wearing black in the movies, but from everything Dillon had told her about Flynn Tanner, he was one of the good guys.

The other man was next to Quincy's chair in a stance that gave Shay the impression he was standing guard. Unlike the other man, this one was a giant. Not only was he the tallest man she had ever seen, he appeared to have muscles on top of muscles. The white T-shirt he wore could have been made from a bed sheet, leaving little material for scraps. Over the T-shirt, he wore a brown suede vest open in the front, a pair of jeans, and black boots fancied by those of the motorcycle gang persuasion. A pair of mirrored sunglasses completed the ensemble, which effectively concealed the color and expression of his eyes.

Dillon came down the ramp as she approached. "Why don't you introduce the dogs to Flynn and Dugan the way you introduced me the first day I arrived at your cabin?"

With about a million questions on the tip of her tongue about his friends, she asked just one. "Where did your friends come from, Thugs Are Us?"

"They might not be very pretty, but I would trust them with my life." His mouth twisted in a rueful smile. "Which is exactly what I'm doing."

Shay called the dogs to her side and asked the two men to shake hands with her.

Dillon made the introductions.

"Shay, this is Flynn Tanner and Dugan Charles."

Each man stepped forward, Flynn first, who took her hand despite the warning growl from the German shepherd.

"It's a pleasure to meet you, Miss Oakland."

She smiled. "We're fairly informal around here. Shay will be fine."

"Miss Oakland will be better," interjected Dillon. Ignoring Flynn's amused expression and Shay's frown, he gestured for Dugan to join them.

Shay's hand disappeared in the large man's grip, which surprised her by being so gentle. With a brief nod, Dugan returned to his earlier stance next to Quincy's wheelchair.

To Shay's utter amazement, Chalk immediately took to the gentle giant and followed him. The dog sat on his haunches next to Dugan. The other two dogs wandered over to her father for the expected pat on the head, then found a spot of shade on the other end of the deck and plopped down for a nap.

Flynn commented, "If they hadn't chased one of my best operatives off Miss Oakland's property, I'd never believe they were guard dogs to see them now." He directed his dark gaze at Shay. "Would they watch over your father with the same intensity as they protect you?"

"I think so, if they thought he was being threatened in any way. You saw how they acted when we arrived here. They don't like strangers, four-legged or two-legged. They have gone after deer with the same enthusiasm they've chased an uninvited visitor. I can't guarantee they would stand guard over Quincy every second of the day, though."

"That's Dugan's job," commented Flynn. "The dogs will be a deterrent for anyone wandering too close to the cabin and a warning system to Dugan."

Shay glanced at her father, who was engrossed in a conversation with the man named Dugan. "Other than his size, what qualifications does the man have to keep my father safe?"

Dillon started to speak but Flynn held his hand up to hold him off. "It's a fair question. Dugan is sort of a jack-of-all-trades and master of all of them. His résumé would make for interesting reading except he couldn't put down much of the things he was involved in with the military because most of what he was assigned to do was classified. He's a third-degree black belt in several forms of martial arts, and there isn't a firearm made that he can't take apart and put together blindfolded. He can also hit whatever he's aiming at."

"It sounds like he's overqualified to be staying with a disabled chief of police on the off chance this guy shows up here."

Dillon provided the answer. "Dugan loves fishing, and he rarely gets an opportunity to throw a hook into the water. He jumped at the chance to spend some time with Quincy when I hinted that the fish in Saber Lake are distant relatives of Moby Dick."

"And he believed you?"

"Probably not, but I've found it takes very little to encourage Dugan to throw a line in the water." As though reading her mind, he added, "There isn't another man besides Flynn I'd want to have on my side in a dangerous situation more than Dugan, Shay. He'll take good care of your father."

Directing her next question to the silent man at Dillon's side, she asked, "You said on the off chance this guy shows. That doesn't sound like you are all that sure he's coming here. How do you even know you have the right man?"

"A hunch led to a fingerprint, which led to Jordan Reinhold. Part of the investigation consisted of going through newspaper files searching for any threats or threatening incidents Dillon might have forgotten about. That's how we found Jordan Reinhold. He had blamed Dillon for getting kicked out of football even though it was Reinhold's fault. We'd eliminated the ex-husband of a woman Dillon had dated. That left us with Jordan Reinhold, who left a fingerprint in Dillon's office.''

''I understand why Dillon should leave the area since you've trailed his enemy to Minnesota, but I don't see why it's necessary for Quincy to be guarded. This guy can't possibly know about us other than the address from the secretary's appointment book is Quincy's. There's no reason for him to harm us.''

''His method of operation so far has been to damage or destroy anything Dillon cares about. His car, his apartment, his office. He even took a potshot at me when I was parking my car near my office one night, evidently because he knows Dillon and I are friends.''

Dillon jerked his head around to face Flynn. ''You never told me that!''

Flynn shrugged. ''He missed. There was nothing to tell.''

Shay saw the dark temper in Dillon's eyes and brought the subject back to the original topic. ''Up until only a few days ago, Dillon didn't even know Quincy or me. Reinhold can't possibly have any idea of our existence other than I work for Dream Street. Why would we be in any danger?''

''You're thinking like a rational person, Miss Oakland. To you, it wouldn't make sense for some nut to destroy another man's possessions, either. This guy does not think like you and I do, which is what makes him so dangerous. We don't know what direction he'll jump next, which is why we brought Dugan here as a bodyguard for your father. We have no way of telling how much Reinhold learned when he broke into Dillon's office. As soon as we get you out of here, we're going to set up a trap to get this maniac.''

She jerked her head around to meet Dillon's gaze. "I thought we were both leaving."

"We talked it over this morning before you got here. Actually, it was Quincy's idea to set a trap and let Reinhold walk into it. He's worked out a plan we all think will work." Dillon put his hand on her arm. "We all agreed this is a perfect opportunity, perhaps the only one we'll get to catch this nut. I don't want to have to keep hiding out the rest of my life, Shay. I want an end to this harassment. I want my life back."

Which meant his life in San Francisco, she realized. "Exactly where am I to go to get out of the way?" Her voice was flat and unemotional.

Dillon didn't like the way she phrased her question, nor the toneless voice she'd used to ask it. But before he could explain the situation better, Quincy rolled his chair to where they were standing near the railing. Dugan walked beside him.

"You've been tied down to caring for me for the past two months, Shay," her father said. "You deserve a vacation and this is a good time to take one.

Your mother is in the Bahamas for a couple of weeks and would love to have you join her there.''

"How do you know that?" she asked, even though she was sure she knew the answer.

"I called her agent this morning and found out where she was. Then I put a call through to her. She's recovering from another bout of plastic surgery so no one knows where she is. There won't be any of those reporters you hate so much. She's staying in a villa overlooking a private beach, and she said there's plenty of room."

"I see," she said softly.

And she did. From Quincy's point of view, her mother's villa was the perfect place to stash Shay out of the way while the boys played cops and robbers. Monica always had her own security staff and because of the swelling and discoloration that always accompanied reconstructive surgery, she wouldn't be seeking any publicity. In fact, the older woman always took great pains to insure no one except a few select people were allowed to know where she was and why. Shay also knew her mother would be bored out of her mind without anyone to entertain her, and Shay could be relied on to keep her silence on the subject of the little nips and tucks Monica had undergone to stave off the lines of time.

Dillon added his own brand of persuasion. "You'll have plenty of uninterrupted time to work on Lady Shay designs while enjoying the Bahamas."

"What more could I ask for?" she murmured. "When am I supposed to leave?"

Flynn glanced at the watch on his wrist. "We booked a flight out of the Duluth airport for four this afternoon. That gives you a couple of hours to pack whatever you need before I drive you to the airport."

Shay gazed silently at Flynn. The private investigator was thorough. She had to give him that much. She was glad, for Dillon's sake, that the man was good at his work. She was in the way, and Flynn had worked out a place to safely send her. He was just doing his job.

She looked at her father. Quincy's eyes were gleaming with excitement. He was clearly in his element. She glanced at Dugan and saw her own reflection in his mirrored sunglasses.

Shay finally met Dillon's gaze. Her stomach was knotted with the tension it was taking for her to remain outwardly calm. She had lost her heart to him within the past couple of days, but her pride was intact and she would be damned if she would lose that, too.

Lifting her chin, she let her gaze include each of the four men. "I'd better get back to my cabin and repack my suitcase, then. The things I packed earlier won't be appropriate for a vacation in the sun. Don't worry, Mr. Tanner," she added as she saw him glance at his watch, "I'll keep the luggage to only one bag, and I'll be back here in plenty of time to leave for the airport."

She turned and walked swiftly down the ramp and across the grass. She was unaware that Flynn grabbed Dillon's arm to stop him from following her. She didn't look back toward the deck as she stepped into Quincy's boat to retrieve the suitcase Dillon had brought with him earlier before the plans had been changed. She untied her boat and started the engine, pushing the throttle full open as she steered the boat toward her cabin.

She didn't allow herself to think about the previous night spent with Dillon. Looking back was not going to be a smart thing to do for a while, possibly for a very long time.

She purposely cut the time short when she returned to Quincy's cabin so there would be little left before she was to leave for the airport. As she tied up her boat on the other side of the dock from her father's boat, she wondered who would be taking care of the two crafts. She wasn't going to worry about it. The boats were probably part of Plan C or D in Flynn's arsenal of strategic tactics, she thought cynically.

When she hefted her suitcase onto the dock, Dillon was there to take it from her.

"Damn it, Shay! Why didn't you answer the radio? I called three times to ask why you were taking so long." He held up Quincy's boat key. "We were about to take your father's boat over to your cabin to check on you."

"I had a few things to do around the cabin since I'm going to be gone for a while."

"You've cut it pretty close. We barely have time to say goodbye."

She stepped onto the dock. "Your friend Flynn was pretty thorough explaining everything, Dillon," she said as she began walking up the dock toward Quincy's cabin. "Did he leave something out you think I should know about?"

"I don't want to talk about the damn plans Flynn's made. I wanted to have a chance to explain that I'm sending you away because I want you to be safe, not because I don't want you with me."

"I'm not giving you a hard time about it, am I?"

"I'd feel better if you would," he admitted. "The way you reacted when Flynn told you about joining your mother in the Bahamas, you acted as though you didn't care one way or the other."

"Would it have made you feel better if I had a tantrum, kicked, and screamed and cried? Would you have relented and let me stay?"

"No. I want you out of here before this joker shows up."

"That's why I didn't waste my breath. My opinion wouldn't have mattered or changed anything, so I kept it to myself." She took several steps, then stopped. "In a way, I'm glad I found out now your views on a relationship, Dillon. The only time you're interested in what I want is when we're in bed. Outside the bedroom, it only matters what you want."

"That's not true, Shay."

"Then why wasn't I included when you were making your plans for the trap? Why wasn't I asked if I would go to the Bahamas instead of having the trip presented to me after all the arrangements were made?"

"We acted on what we thought was the best to insure your safety."

The dogs ran down the grassy slope to greet Shay and she fussed over them until they were satisfied and ambled off. Shay glanced toward the cabin. The deck was empty, but she could see Flynn's tall figure watching them from the other side of the screen door.

Shay continued walking, reaching the ramp a few steps ahead of Dillon. She felt his fingers close around her upper arm to halt her progress.

"Let go of me, Dillon. I have a plane to catch, remember?"

Keeping his voice low, he bent his head to speak close to her ear. "When this is over, you and I are going to have a long talk about what we both want, and I don't mean just in bed."

"When this is over, you will be returning to your life in San Francisco, Dillon. We both knew that from the beginning. I told you last night, there would be no regrets, no recriminations, and I meant what I said. I've never expected any promises you can't keep and I haven't made any to you."

The screen door slid open and Flynn stepped out. "We need to get going, Miss Oakland, if we're going to make your flight."

"I'm ready," she said quietly, afraid to say anything else for fear of losing the tight control she had over her emotions. She was determined that the last memory Dillon would have of her would be of a woman with her chin held high and proud, not a blubbering idiot crying her eyes out. That would come later when she was alone.

Flynn relieved her of her suitcase. "Your father wants to see you before you leave."

Shay nodded, but didn't move away from Dillon. She couldn't leave with Dillon angry. He needed to have his thoughts on his enemy, not be dwelling on his anger.

She placed her hand on the side of Dillon's face. "I hope everything works out all right for you," she said quietly. "And I hope you catch this guy so your life can get back to normal."

Anger flickered in his eyes. "That sounds very much like goodbye."

"Whether your trap works or not, you'll be leaving this area. I guess it is goodbye."

"You're wrong. Have you forgotten what I said last night about beginnings and not endings? We started something I don't plan on giving up."

Flynn called again from the doorway, this time not bothering to soften his impatience. "Miss Oakland! Could you get a move on?"

"I can see why you and he are friends, Dillon," she said dryly. "You both have such a way with words."

"Shay, I'm serious. About us, about what we have together, about not ending our relationship."

"Let's get this guy out of your life first before we talk about bringing me into it."

He followed her into the cabin. "You are in it."

She shook her head as she opened the screen door. "No, I'm the one leaving on a flight to the Bahamas by popular demand, remember?"

As soon as he saw her, Quincy beckoned for Shay to come over to the desk where he was seated in his wheelchair, staring at a small monitor of some kind on the desktop. Dillon stayed just inside the door, his gaze never leaving her as she walked toward her father.

Shay bent down to study the jiggly lines dancing horizontally across the screen. "What is that?"

"Either the motion detector or the meter that will let us know if someone is coming down the lane. There's a gadget over there—" he pointed toward a small television screen behind the monitor "—that shows any boat traffic on the lake. I watched you arrive."

Shay glanced at her father. "Are they really expecting someone to approach the cabin from the lake?"

Quincy chuckled. "I tried to tell them there are only two access roads to the lake—one is your lane and the other is mine. I also informed them that there is no way for anyone to launch a boat onto the lake except from next to the boathouse. Dugan is setting up another camera in one of the trees near the launching ramp. Why anyone would want to put a boat in the lake a hundred yards from my cabin in order to approach the cabin by boat skips right over my sense of logic."

Shay caught the glitter of amusement in his eyes. "You're enjoying this, aren't you? All the fuss, all this state-of-the-art equipment."

"They mean well," he said, keeping his voice low, "but this is the country, not the big city. I can't seem to get across to them that we do things a little different out here."

Shay detected something other than amusement in her father's eyes. "Exactly what are you up to, Quincy? And if you tell me not to worry my pretty little head about it, I'll hide your stash of whiskey you don't think I know about."

He gave her a look of horror and started talking. "I made a few phone calls to the office. That's all. Brad's on the lookout for any cars with rental plates that pass through Cadance. I've alerted Travis to keep an eye out for the same thing at the gas station. Doris will let me know if she has any customers asking questions about us or asking for directions to the cabin. If they spot this guy, we'll have a little advance warning."

"Your idea makes more sense than all these high-tech gadgets. If a deer comes across one of their sensor things, he's going to set off a hell of a ruckus."

"It could get real exciting around here with all the beeps and bleeps going off. I'm looking forward to it."

"What is the real reason you want me out of here, Quincy? You've never been particularly concerned for my safety when I've gone out on calls for you. You know I can take care of myself and won't do anything stupid. Why send me off to hold Monica's hand while her sutures heal?"

Quincy looked past her to where Dillon was stepping out onto the deck behind Flynn. Lowering his voice even though it was doubtful the two men could hear him, he said, "You're of legal age, Shay. No one can tell you where or when to go if you don't choose to go. I do believe you could use a vacation, but listening to Monica's horror stories of every snip and tuck would be more of a punishment than a vacation. I think you should drive yourself to the airport instead of bothering Mr. Tanner." Chuckling, he added, "He could string a thousand more feet of wire in the time it would take him to drive you to Duluth. I'll remind him of that after I tell him you decided to take your truck. Doris could use some help looking out for our friend."

Shay didn't hesitate. She bent forward and kissed her father's cheek. "I suppose the phones are bugged."

"Probably. I wouldn't take the chance."

Shay straightened and hitched the strap of her purse over her shoulder. "Will any cannons go off or rocket launchers fire at me when I drive down the lane?"

"I don't think so. Only one way to find out."

She started for the side door that led to where her truck was parked. When she reached the truck, a quick glance in the back reassured her Flynn had put her cases there. As she started the engine and backed out of her space, she put the truck in gear and wished she could be a fly on a wall when all hell broke loose inside the cabin when Flynn and Dillon discovered she had left.

Dillon was standing in a threatening stance in front of Quincy's wheelchair, his legs parted, his hands clamped on his hips, and his back bent to bring his face closer to the older man's.

"What the hell do you mean, Shay's gone?"

"You and Mr. Tanner were busy so she decided to drive herself to the airport. I don't see what you're getting so het up about. You didn't want her here and she's gone. I would think that would make you happy."

"I didn't want her going anywhere by herself. Who knows what Reinhold would do to her if he found out how important she is to me?"

Quincy's gaze narrowed. "Exactly how would this fellow learn that when she doesn't know it?"

Dillon's threatening manner disappeared, to be replaced by an expression of confusion on his face as he straightened. "Of course she knows it."

"Have you told her?"

"Not in those exact words, but she should be able to read between the lines."

Chuckling, Quincy picked up the fishing reel in his lap and continued filling it with fresh line. "If there is a woman alive who can read between the lines of anything a man says, I want to meet her. Hell, I'll even marry her. Women like to hear the words in very clear English without any doubt at all about their meaning. There's another little thing you'd better know about my daughter. Growing up without a mother has made her more independent than other young women her age. She's not the meek pipe-and-slippers-fetching type."

"Hell, I know that, Quincy. I wouldn't want her any other way than she is."

Quincy quirked an eyebrow. "Was that the impression you were trying to make when you told her to hightail it to her momma's before things got rough? I've taught her to never back down from a fight. Running away isn't setting too good with her."

"I want her safe, Quincy. As her father, I would think you would want the same thing."

Setting down the reel, Quincy gave Dillon his full attention. "During the last couple of days, you've taught me a great deal about selfish pride. Now I'm going to throw your own words back at you. You said my pride was coming between Shay and me, that I hated needing her help but that she thrived on feeling needed. She has her own share of pride, you know. Pride leaves a hollow place deep inside that love fills up if we let it."

"I don't remember saying that last part."

"That's my contribution."

Dillon took a couple of steps away, then back again, only to turn and retrace his path on the wooden floor. "This is the damnedest conversation to be having with a woman's father, especially when the father knows I've slept with his daughter."

"That's how I knew how Shay felt about you. She would never have allowed you in her bed if she didn't love you. That part's easy to figure out. How you feel about her is still a puzzle to both her and me."

Dillon stopped walking suddenly and stared at the older man. "You're kidding, right? I've never had a woman run me through a wringer as often and as well as she does and still come back for more. Flynn accuses me of having a sappy look on my face every time I look at her. He even said he could tell when I'm thinking about her just by my expression."

"Humph. Here I thought that was your normal look."

"If I leave right now, do you think I could catch her at the airport before her plane takes off?"

Quincy shook his head emphatically. "No."

"Why not? She only left a little while ago. I could probably catch up with her on the road and bring her back."

"Not if you take the route to Duluth."

Dillon's eyes narrowed. He became very still. "Exactly what are you saying, Quincy? That she's not on her way to the airport, after all?"

"I doubt it. If she was in danger, would *you* merrily hop on a plane to go soak in the sun until the danger was over?"

"That's different, and you know it."

"No, I don't. I can't speak from experience since I've never been married, but you mentioned your parents one night when we were playing poker. They evidently had a close relationship, one built on love and trust. You even said that after the shock of their death, you realized you were glad they had died together because it would be too difficult for one to live without the other. I'd like my daughter to have that type of relationship with a man."

The phone near the sofa rang and Flynn yanked open the sliding-screen door to enter the room. Quincy rolled his chair to the phone and waited for Flynn's nod before he picked up the receiver. His gaze was on the tape recorder next to the phone as he said, "Hello?"

A few seconds later he said, "I'm doing fine, Doris. How about you? You still giving Murray a hard time?"

Keeping his voice low, Dillon explained to Flynn who Doris was, and both men started to walk toward the door to the deck when they heard a different note in Quincy's voice as he responded to something the woman was telling him.

"Now that is interesting." His voice hardened suddenly. "What the hell is she doing talking to him?" A short time later he ordered, "You tell her to get her butt back into the kitchen with Murray and his meat cleaver. Give the guy the directions he's asking for and get him out of there as quickly as you can without making him suspicious. What kind of car is this guy driving, Doris?''

After a brief pause, he repeated what the waitress said for Flynn's and Dillon's sake. "He's driving a black, four-door sedan. That's a big help.'' He continued with his instructions. "After he's gone, call my office and have Jewel get on the radio to Brad to tell him to park the patrol car across the entrance to my lane after Brad sees the suspect's car enter my lane. Tell him not to stay with the squad car but to find a place in the woods where he'll be able to see the lane and to take his small radio with him.''

Flynn and Dillon were hovering over Quincy like two hawks eyeing an intended victim they were about ready to tear apart.

After Quincy murmured, "Thanks, Doris,'' and hung up the receiver, it was Dillon who stated, "Reinhold's at Murray's Café, isn't he?''

Quincy nodded and said, "And he'll be on his way here once Doris gives him the directions. That gives us time to prepare our little surprises. It will take him about ten minutes to make it from Murray's to the entrance of my lane. Another four or five minutes for him to drive to the cabin. Brad will close the back door, so to speak. It's up to you guys to put your plan in motion.''

Flynn didn't wait around to ask how this woman at the café knew about Jordan Reinhold. Questions would come later after they had the man in custody. He left the cabin to notify Dugan that the shark was about to slip into the net.

Dillon wasn't going to wait. "The woman who was talking to Reinhold, whose butt you wanted back in the kitchen, was Shay, wasn't it?"

"Yeah," Quincy answered with a heartfelt sigh. "It's a darn shame she's too old to give a good paddling for sticking her neck out by talking to the creep. We're going to have to postpone any recriminations until later. We haven't got much time before the fellow gets here."

Quincy was wrong. They had plenty of time. The guy never showed.

Chapter Twelve

Shay was relieved Murray had the good sense not to put her to work doing anything with a knife the way her hands were shaking. Washing fresh spinach leaves was boring but at least she couldn't do much damage to herself. If only she knew what was happening at the cabin, she would be able to relax. Her nerves were dancing even more frantically after she'd talked to the man who had been stalking Dillon.

Her first impression had been of an average, good-looking man who had a pleasant smile. When she served the glass of iced tea he'd ordered, she noticed his polite smile wasn't reflected in his eyes. There didn't seem to be any expression at all in the depths of his dark eyes, except when he asked if she knew where

Quincy McCall lived. She wouldn't have thought dark eyes could look like cold ice, but his did.

Stalling by saying she was new to the area, she called Doris over and had the man repeat his question to the waitress. Without blinking an eye, Doris had told the man that it was time for her to call home and check in with her baby-sitter. If he didn't mind waiting a few minutes, she would give him the directions after she had called home.

While Doris used the pay phone across the room, Shay tried to appear as though nothing was out of the ordinary as she wiped off the counter and made polite conversation so he wouldn't be able to hear Doris's side of the phone call. Since Doris's idea of a whisper resembled air escaping from ten balloons, Shay couldn't be sure Reinhold didn't hear Doris's comments, which had nothing to do with baby-sitters or children.

To her utter amazement, Dillon's enemy started coming on to her, asking what was a nice girl like her doing in a place like this and what time did she get off work. He said he had some business to take care of that would take an hour or so, then he was free for the rest of the day. He suggested she show him around town later and he would make it worth her while by taking her out to dinner.

Shay had wrung out the rag in the sink under the counter with a lot more vigor than necessary, wishing it was Reinhold's neck, as she declined his offer as graciously as she could. Looking back, Shay admitted she had no acting ability at all. Even though he showed no reaction, Shay was afraid her feelings toward him were too apparent. His "business" could end Dillon's life if anything went wrong at the cabin. Shay couldn't separate that horrendous fact by play-acting.

Luckily Doris returned just in time to stop Shay from doing anything stupid like hitting him over the head with the coffeepot. Doris gave him the directions to Quincy's cabin. With a wink in Shay's direction, he left the diner.

Doris complained that he hadn't even left a tip, then proceeded to tell Shay what Quincy had said. Everything was under control so Shay was instructed to go into the kitchen and help Murray while they waited to hear what happened at the cabin.

The minute hand on the clock on one of the kitchen walls seemed to crawl around the large circular face as Shay waited. And waited.

Every time Murray dropped a lid back onto a pot or banged a spoon against the edge of a pan, Shay felt like throwing something at him. Her nerves jangled enough all on their own without any help from his sound effects. Shay had never thought of the diner as being an especially noisy place other than Doris's ear-splitting conversations. Now every sound seemed magnified. Doris yelled her orders through an open section of the wall where dishes were placed on a shelf for her to take to the customers. There was the normal buzz of conversation coming from the dining area and Murray's kitchen chorus of clatter and clang.

The startling sound of glass shattering was too loud to be a dropped drinking glass or a plate. Shay glanced at Murray, who was looking at the swinging door. Instead of coming into the kitchen to get the broom, Doris yelled Murray's name.

As he started drying off his hands, Shay offered, "I'll go clean up the glass if you want me to, Murray, so you can keep up with the lunch orders."

He shook his head. "It must be more than a couple of broken glasses. Doris would have swept those up herself. I think it was one of the big windows in front."

Shay didn't like the sound of that. It would require more than gravel spun up onto the glass to make the large panes break.

With the tap running in the sink in front of her, she didn't hear the diner's back door open.

When Murray didn't return right away to get the broom and dustpan, Shay decided to go see what was happening in the dining room. She started to turn off the running water when a large hand clamped over her mouth and a soft, male voice warned, "Keep those pretty lips shut, babe."

Her hands were wet and dripping water as she raised them to attempt to drag the hand away from her mouth. She made a muffled sound of protest when he began to drag her toward the back door.

Behind the diner was an industrial-size Dumpster and a stack of plastic milk cases. Those things were supposed to be there. The huge motorcycle ten feet from the back door looked vaguely familiar. Then she remembered why.

Jordan Reinhold loosened the pressure of his hand over her mouth. "I'm going to take my hand away. If you scream, you won't be able to say anything for a long time. It's up to you."

She nodded her assent, and he dropped his hand. His gaze roamed over her. "Our mutual friend can pick them. You're quite a looker, babe. Dillon always has had an eye for the women."

In a bored tone, she asked, "Am I supposed to know who you're talking about?"

He chuckled. "Knowing his reputation, you know him very well, babe. You can put away the dumb act. You know Street, and you know who I am. You gave yourself away by using my name when you told me to come back again sometime after the big-mouthed waitress gave me directions to McCall's cabin."

Shay closed her eyes briefly, cursing herself for making such a stupid mistake.

He pulled her roughly over to the motorcycle. "We're going for a little ride and you're going to tell me what kind of reception my old buddy has waiting for me."

"What makes you think I'm going to tell you anything?"

His fingers tightened around her wrist and she cried out in pain. "You'll tell me, sweet thing. Now climb on the motorcycle. We're going for a little ride."

"This motorcycle belongs to Sandy Knutsen. His older brother is a deputy with the Cadance police department. Stealing it was a big mistake."

They both heard the voices from the kitchen, especially Doris's. The waitress had discovered Shay was missing.

The motorcycle's engine roared and the tires spun on the gravel as Reinhold put it in gear. Shay had no choice except to hold on to Dillon's enemy or fall off. Shay heard Reinhold curse under his breath as they went around the corner of the diner. Leaning to one side so she could see around him, Shay saw a large truck blocking the driveway. It was Quincy's truck.

She glanced around the parking lot and the trees on the other side. Dillon was here. She could feel it.

She almost fell off when Reinhold spun the motorcycle around. Murray and Doris were standing in the back doorway of the diner, both helpless to do anything to the driver of the motorcycle with Shay sitting so close. A cloud of dust followed in their wake as Reinhold aimed the motorcycle at the driveway on the other side of the diner.

There was an opening until they were twenty feet away. A tan rental car backed across the driveway entrance, closing the opening. The only way Reinhold could get out would be to try to jump over the car. The truck blocking the other exit was too high.

When Shay realized Reinhold was actually going to attempt it, she yelled, "You fool!" as he stopped to stare at the car.

His hands twisted the controls, revving up the engine loudly.

"Street's not going to have everything he wants. Not this time. He's certainly not going to want you after you smash into that car."

Shay knew that nothing she said would change his mind. She also realized that Dillon, Flynn and Dugan wouldn't rush Reinhold as long as she was on the motorcycle. Since she didn't like the option of smashing into the car, she knew what she had to do.

She had to get off the motorcycle.

She waited until he had released the brake, sending the large motorcycle toward the parked car. She brought her leg up to the padded seat and pushed away with her hands at the same time as she kicked with her foot. She went flying off the back of the motorcycle, hitting the ground hard before rolling several times over the gravel driveway.

Familiar hands turned her over to lay on her back. She looked up and saw Dillon bending over her.

"I'm all right," she insisted. "Go get Reinhold."

Doris knelt down on the other side of Shay. When Dillon didn't move, the older woman snapped, "Do you want that bastard to come back and run over her next time?"

With one last glance, Dillon got to his feet just as the sound of a huge crash and explosion reached them.

"Take care of her, Doris," he said grimly. Then he walked away.

* * *

Doris treated Shay's skinned elbow with a generous application of iodine and a gauze bandage. The waitress kept exclaiming what a miracle it was that Shay only had the one injury and it was minor.

Doris had taken her to the kitchen, well away from the burning car and motorcycle. She had heard the fire engines and Murray had popped in to tell her that a large giant had driven Quincy's truck to the cabin and brought the chief of police back with him to the crime scene.

Shay had caught a glimpse of Flynn through the swinging door. He was examining the broken window. Shay learned from Murray that Reinhold had thrown a brick through the window to draw Murray out of the kitchen. His intent had been to either take Shay as hostage or to hurt Dillon by harming her. They would never know which. The body recovered from the crash site wouldn't be hurting anyone ever again.

Shay caught glimpses of everyone except Dillon.

The word had spread quickly around town and the parking lot filled up with the curious and, to Murray's delight, the hungry citizens of Cadance. After the firemen had put out the blaze, they trooped into the diner, too.

Doris was having a great time detailing her part in the event, her participation growing each time she told it. Murray was back at the stove by demand of the hungry crowd.

The spinach leaves were where she'd left them in the colander in the sink. She turned the water on again and proceeded to wash the leaves. She was in no hurry to go into the diner where she would be expected to answer a lot of questions. She wasn't ready to see the burned car or the motorcycle yet either.

She heard the hinges on the swinging door squeak, but didn't look up, expecting it to be Doris bringing in a load of dirty dishes. When she felt large strong hands clamp around her waist, she knew it wasn't Doris.

Dillon turned her around and brought his hands up to cup her face. "Don't you ever scare me like that again, Shay Oakland, or I promise I'll take a pair of your father's handcuffs and secure one of your wrists to mine and throw away the key in order to keep you safe."

She opened her mouth to explain, but he covered her lips roughly with his own. Her wet hands left dark imprints on the front of his shirt, but he didn't seem to notice. She didn't, either. Nor did she realize a dripping spinach leaf was stuck to the back of her hand.

Dillon took her mouth with all the hunger, fear and passion built up to a fiery heat during the past hour. If he'd had any doubts about how he felt about Shay, they had been eliminated when he'd seen her on the motorcycle behind Reinhold. She'd been only inches away from the man who had tried to kill him. If Reinhold had known how important she was... Dillon slanted his mouth over hers to deepen the assault on her mouth to drive away the thoughts of what could have happened to her.

Shay made a startled cry when she was suddenly hoisted off her feet and flung over a large muscular shoulder.

Murray took exception to the unusual treatment of his temporary kitchen help. "Hey, buddy. What the hell you think you're doing?"

"That's a question I've asked myself ever since I met this woman," grumbled Dillon. "If you're going to do anything with that big knife, I wouldn't try it. I've had a rough day and I'm a little cranky."

Doris burst into the kitchen. When she saw the position Shay was in, she let out a laugh that created ripples in the pot of soup. "Well, girl. It looks like the dragon has been vanquished and the hero is about to claim the fair maiden."

"Are you going to let him treat me like a sack of potatoes?" asked Shay from her upside down position. "Do something."

Doris started applauding.

"Thank you very much, Doris," muttered Shay. "That's a big help."

Laughing even harder and louder, Doris held the swinging door open for Dillon. "Guess you won't be staying for lunch. Murray made a terrific lemon meringue pie."

Dillon leaned over and gave Doris a brief kiss on her rouged cheek, astonished when he saw a pinkish tinge creep up her neck. "Not today. Thanks for taking care of Shay, Doris."

"I hope you plan on sticking around awhile, Maverick. Things certainly have perked up around here since you arrived."

Walking toward the entrance of the diner, Dillon said, "Well, don't count on any more excitement. I could use a few dull days after today."

Doris ran ahead to open the door for Dillon since his hands were occupied at the moment. Glancing at the woman bent over his shoulder, Doris grinned. "I think the excitement isn't over yet. You're going to have your hands full in more ways than one before the day is over."

Dillon grinned at her. "I'm counting on it."

Doris stood in the doorway and watched Dillon open the driver's side of Shay's truck and dump Shay onto the seat. He lifted her over the gears between the two bucket seats and maintained a grip on her wrist as he maneuvered his long length behind the steering wheel. A few seconds later the truck sped out of the parking lot and disappeared from view. The waitress's curiosity was aroused when she realized Dillon had turned left instead of right, which would have taken them back to Quincy's cabin. Evidently, the Maverick wanted some privacy.

With a long, deep sigh of contentment, Doris let the door close and returned to her customers.

Inside the truck, Dillon released her wrist and ordered, "Do up your seat belt."

Shay removed the spinach leaf from the back of her hand and rolled the window down enough to toss it out. Then she fastened her seat belt. "Is it over?"

"According to your father, some paperwork has to be filled out, but our part is finished."

"I know," she said, her voice cracking slightly.

He reached over and removed another drop of moisture from her cheek. He asked softly, "Then why the tears? Did I hurt you when I carried you out of Murray's Café?"

She shook her head, not trusting her voice to speak at the moment.

"Then tell me what's wrong."

Her voice was ragged and so low Dillon had to strain to hear her. "I was so afraid he would get to you somehow even with all the precautions. If he'd killed you..." She choked and couldn't finish what she was going to say.

Dillon pulled the truck off the road and shoved the gear into Park. With one hand, he pushed his seat back while the other unfastened her seat belt. Using both hands, he lifted her over the console and onto his lap. He cradled her closely in his arms and felt his shirt dampen with her tears. His fingers soothed and stroked gently over her back. The extent of her distress amazed and humbled him while filling him with such joy. She had to care for him to feel such anguish at the possibility of his being in danger.

As her tears began to subside, she moved her hand over the hard muscles of his chest. She loved the feel of him against her, over her, inside her. No other man could ever take her to the crest of pleasure but Dillon. No other man's touch could fire her blood and make her feel the full joy of being a woman. Only he could make a rainy day sunny and each day a miracle.

Dillon sensed the change in her and his body responded. "Shay," he murmured. "We can't. Not here."

"I know." She sighed heavily. "That's not why I'm touching you. I just need to know you're okay. If I can feel you under my hands, I know you're really all right."

He was definitely more uncomfortable than he'd been a moment ago. His jeans were certainly a good deal tighter than they'd been. If he was going to carry out his plans, he was going to have to put some distance between them. He almost lost his train of thought when she groaned in protest as he lifted her back to her seat.

He laid his wrist over the top of the steering wheel as he turned partially in his seat to face her. "I've made some mistakes with you that I'll try not to make again. One of them is charging ahead with plans that include you without talking to you about them first. I was just about to do it again when we left Murray's, mainly because I was afraid if I gave you a choice, you wouldn't want to go with me."

"So that's why the caveman treatment?"

"Aside from the fact I rather enjoyed it, yes, I suppose it is."

Shay smiled. "I admit I enjoyed it, too. Go on with these plans I might or might not like. Since we're headed in the opposite direction from Saber Lake, I guessed we weren't going back to Quincy's or to my cabin."

He shook his head. "I've seen where you live. I've met your family. I thought it was time you see where I live and meet my sister. I was heading toward the airport. Then I thought we'd discuss how we could combine our lives. With computers, fax machines, and airplanes, I can still run the companies in San Francisco from here if you don't want to leave your father. Although with Dugan staying on permanently, you won't need to be solely responsible for his care."

"Dugan is staying on here?" she asked in astonishment. "When did that happen?"

"He and your father have decided to open a branch of Good Sports in Saber Lake, specializing in fishing equipment." He took her hand. "Quincy called Travis to ask him to look for a specially designed van for the physically challenged so Quincy can get back and forth to the store."

Shay leaned back heavily against the seat. "A week ago I couldn't even persuade him to get dressed. Now he's talking about opening up a sporting goods store."

"And he's happier," added Dillon gently. "You were there for him when he needed you, but he's ready to try it on his own now."

"I'm happy for him. I really am, but he still can't manage to live on his own, Dillon. It's a fact of life there are certain things he will never be physically able to do on his own.''

Dillon tapped his fingers lightly against the steering wheel thoughtfully. ''Well . . .''

''There's more? Please don't tell me Doris is moving in with Quincy. That would be too much.''

Grinning, Dillon enjoyed that thought, too. ''Dugan is moving in.''

''Moving in?''

''His work for Flynn is just the occasional odd job. He said he's getting burned out and wants to enjoy life more while he still has some left. He'll be good for Quincy. He won't take any crap from him and he'll help him learn how to cope with his disability without making it look like he's helping.''

Shay stared at him. For a very long time. Dillon couldn't read her expression and hadn't the faintest idea as to what she was thinking.

Then she ordered, ''Get out of the truck.''

''What?''

''Get out of the truck, Dillon. We're going to take a little walk.''

''We are?'' At least he was being included. For a minute there, he thought he might be walking back to Quincy's alone. ''Where are we going?''

''You'll find out when we get there, city boy.''

Just to be on the safe side, Dillon took the keys with him and shoved them in his pocket as he walked around the front of the truck. Shay was waiting for him. When he approached, she held out her hand and he gladly enclosed her fingers in his.

Instead of drawing him close to her as he had expected and hoped, she started walking down the dirt-and weed-covered incline at the side of the road. She took her time descending the slope, in deference to his bad knee, he guessed.

At the bottom, there was a path of sorts, about wide enough to handle narrow bicycle tires but a tight fit for two adults. Since Shay still retained a firm grip on his hand, Dillon was left to follow behind her. Again she kept the pace leisurely, giving him plenty of time to look out for any surprises that might trip him up.

Just when he was about ready to ask how much farther they had to go, Shay stepped into a clearing where sunlight highlighted a small pond and soft grass. Other than the twitter of a couple of birds, there was no other sound of habitation. It was as though they were the only two people in the world, which is exactly the way Dillon preferred it.

A tree that had been dead perhaps fifty years extended out into the pond about ten feet, a perfect place to sit and dangle feet in the water.

Dillon soon discovered this is exactly what Shay planned to do. The bark had long been worn off the log and its sides were smooth and gray with age and wide enough to make walking on it fairly easy. Near the end, Shay stopped, let go of his hand, and casually stepped around him so he was at the end and she was blocking his retreat.

She sat down and proceeded to take off her shoes and socks, sucking in her breath when she put her bare feet into the cold water. She didn't pressure Dillon into doing the same, leaving it up to him whether he wanted to join her or not.

When he lowered his bare feet into the water, he brought them back out again quickly. "Is this some sort of initiation rite I have to go through before you tell me what we're doing here?"

"It's just something I usually do when I come here." She looked out over the lake. "This is my thinking spot. I've made some major decisions sitting here with my feet in the water with only the birds and fish for company."

Dillon slowly eased his feet back into the water beside hers. He discovered, once his toes were numb, the experience wasn't so bad, after all. "Is the decision you're trying to make whether to come to San Francisco with me or not?"

"No. I'm going. What I need to decide is if I can accept being described under photographs of us as Dillon Street and an unnamed woman. Or even worse, another beauty escorted by the debonair Dillon Street."

"I've never been called debonair in my life."

"You know what I mean. You know how I feel about the celebrity part of your life, but I can't expect you to become a hermit and never go out in public just because I'm not comfortable with the attention you draw from the press. It goes back to not wanting

to be one of the long list of women you've been asso-
ciated with in the past." She stared down at her foot
as she moved it back and forth in the water. "I'm also
having a little trouble adjusting to the fact that I'm
willing to even put up with all that just to be able to be
with you. It's been a little hard on my pride to have to
admit that."

To see her better Dillon changed his position by
shifting one leg over the log. He gently placed a couple of fingers under her chin but needed to add pressure to urge her to look at him.

"I don't have any problems admitting I want to be
with you. The logistics of where and how can be
worked out now that I know you feel the same. As for
the publicity pictures, there won't be that many. It will
be a long time before I feel like sharing my wife with
the rest of the world."

Shay was so startled, she almost slid off the log, but
Dillon caught her. Grinning down at her, he pulled her
closer, easing her legs over his thighs. "I guess you
weren't expecting the part about being a wife yet."

Her eyes were still wide with surprise, her skin pale.
Lifting a hand to the side of his face, she wasn't at all
surprised to find her fingers were shaking. "I wasn't
expecting that word at all. You never... I mean, we
haven't... Are you sure, Dillon? It would kill me if
you're joking."

He pulled her into his arms and sighed deeply when
she buried her face in the hollow of his throat.
"There's nothing remotely funny about the way you

make me feel, Lady Shay. I can't point to any one moment and say that's when I fell in love with you. Lord knows, I felt as though I'd been struck by lightning the first moment I saw you, and I haven't recovered yet."

He lifted her chin so she would look at him. He brushed her mouth with his, lightly, briefly, the electric current of the magic between them setting off flares of desire throughout his whole body.

"I have to know how you feel about me. I know you think that we haven't known each other very long and that we don't have much in common except a powerful physical attraction, but we have so much more. We have the rest of our lives to find out everything else."

Shay slid her arms around his neck and kissed him with all the pent-up passion deep inside her. He responded instantly, breaking away from her mouth briefly.

"Say yes," he demanded.

"Yes, what?" she murmured dreamily as she nibbled on his throat, his jawline, just below his ear, irrationally pleased when he shuddered against her.

"Yes, you'll marry me. Yes, you will love me forever. Yes, you'll be the mother of my children. Yes, you'll grow old with me."

"How long do I have to think about it?" she asked, leaning back against his arms.

Dillon let her weight carry her down to the log and he went with her until he was lying over her. "You have about two seconds."

He took her mouth with a deep hunger as ravenous as a starving man and as tender as a man in love. Her immediate response heightened his own and her loving generosity overwhelmed him.

"Yes," she sighed as he slid his hands over her body, lingering, clasping, smoothing, stroking, fanning the flames to a roaring blaze.

Buttons came undone and zippers lowered. Soft murmurs of need were spoken between kisses that became more demanding. Dillon knew he wasn't going to last long before he had to have her. Knowing she would be his forever made him want to claim her completely.

But there was one thing he needed to say before he slid into her. "Shay, if I manage this without both of us falling into the water and drowning, I don't want to hear you call me city boy anymore."

"It's a deal," she said breathlessly, her hands stroking possessively over his muscular back. "And you don't need to worry about snapping turtles if we do fall in. They stay close to the bottom when it's this cold."

Dillon lifted his head and looked down at her. "Snapping turtles?"

"Don't worry. I'll protect you."

Shay lifted her hips into his hard body and covered his mouth with hers. Soon Dillon lost all thought of anything else but her.

* * * * *

**Rugged and lean...and the best-looking,
sweetest-talking men to be found in the
entire Lone Star state!**

*Diana
Palmer*

LONG, TALL TEXANS

In July 1994, Silhouette is very proud to bring you
Diana Palmer's first three LONG, TALL TEXANS.
CALHOUN, JUSTIN and TYLER—the three cowboys
who started the legend. Now they're back by popular
demand in one classic volume—and they're ready to
lasso your heart! Beautifully repackaged for this
special event, this collection is sure to be a
longtime keepsake!

"Diana Palmer makes a reader want to find a Texan
of her own to love!"   —*Affaire de Coeur*

**LONG, TALL TEXANS—the first three—
reunited in this special roundup!**

**Available in July,
wherever Silhouette books are sold.**

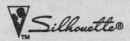

Take 4 bestselling love stories FREE

Plus get a FREE surprise gift!

Special Limited-time Offer

Mail to Silhouette Reader Service™

3010 Walden Avenue
P.O. Box 1867
Buffalo, N.Y. 14269-1867

YES! Please send me 4 free Silhouette Special Edition® novels and my free surprise gift. Then send me 6 brand-new novels every month, which I will receive months before they appear in bookstores. Bill me at the low price of $2.89 each plus 25¢ delivery and applicable sales tax, if any.* That's the complete price and—compared to the cover prices of $3.50 each—quite a bargain! I understand that accepting the books and gift places me under no obligation ever to buy any books. I can always return a shipment and cancel at any time. Even if I never buy another book from Silhouette, the 4 free books and the surprise gift are mine to keep forever.

235 BPA ANRQ

Name	(PLEASE PRINT)	
Address	Apt. No.	
City	State	Zip

This offer is limited to one order per household and not valid to present Silhouette Special Edition® subscribers. *Terms and prices are subject to change without notice. Sales tax applicable in N.Y.

USPED-94R

©1990 Harlequin Enterprises Limited

BABY BLESSED
Debbie Macomber

Molly Larabee didn't expect her reunion with estranged husband Jordan to be quite so explosive. Their tumultuous past was filled with memories of tragedy—and love. Rekindling familiar passions left Molly with an unexpected blessing...and suddenly a future with Jordan was again worth fighting for!

Don't miss Debbie Macomber's fiftieth book, BABY BLESSED, available in July!

She's friend, wife, mother—she's you! And beside each **Special Woman** stands a wonderfully *special* man. It's a celebration of our heroines— and the men who become part of their lives.

TSW794

by Christine Rimmer

**Three rapscallion brothers. Their main talent: making trouble.
Their only hope: three uncommon women who knew the way to
heal a wounded heart! Meet them in these books:**

Jared Jones

hadn't had it easy with women. Retreating to his mountain cabin, he found willful
Eden Parker waiting to show him a good woman's love in MAN OF THE MOUNTAIN
(May, SE #886).

Patrick Jones

was determined to show Regina Black that a wild Jones boy was *not* husband
material. But that wouldn't stop her from trying to nab him in SWEETBRIAR SUMMIT
(July, SE #896)

Jack Roper

came to town looking for the wayward and beautiful Olivia Larrabee. He never
suspected he'd uncover a long-buried Jones family secret in A HOME FOR THE HUNTER
(September, SE #908)....

**Meet these rascal men and the women who'll tame them,
only from Silhouette Books and Special Edition!**

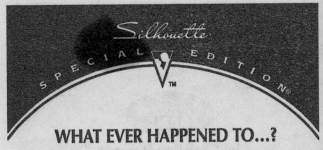

WHAT EVER HAPPENED TO...?

Have you been wondering when much-loved characters will finally get their own stories? Well, have we got a lineup for you! Silhouette Special Edition is proud to present a *Spin-off Spectacular!* Be sure to catch these exciting titles from some of your favorite authors:

HOMEWARD BOUND (July, SE #900) Mara Anvik is recalled to her old home for a dire mission—which reunites her with old flame Mark Toovak in *Sierra Rydell*'s exciting spin-off to ON MIDDLE GROUND (SE #772).

BABY, COME BACK (August, SE #903) Erica Spindler returns with an emotional story about star-crossed lovers Hayes Bradford and Alice Dougherty, who are given a second chance for marriage in this follow-up to BABY MINE (SE #728).

THE WEDDING KNOT (August, SE #905) Pamela Toth's tie-in to WALK AWAY, JOE (SE #850) features a marriage of convenience that allows Daniel Sixkiller to finally adopt...and to find his perfect mate in determined Karen Whitworth!

A RIVER TO CROSS (September, SE #910) Shane Macklin and Tina Henderson shared a forbidden passion, which they can no longer deny in the latest tale from *Laurie Paige*'s WILD RIVER series.

Don't miss these wonderful titles, only for our readers— only from Silhouette Special Edition!